AN A CIRCUIT NOVEL

GEORGINA BLOOMBERG
& CATHERINE HAPKA

BLOOMSBURY
NEW YORK   LONDON   NEW DELHI   SYDNEY

To Henry.
Thank you for letting me accomplish
more than I ever dared to dream of
—G. B.

First published in the United States of America in August 2013
by Bloomsbury Children's Books
www.bloomsbury.com

For information about permission to reproduce selections from this book, write to
Permissions, Bloomsbury Children's Books, 1385 Broadway, New York, New York 10018
Bloomsbury books may be purchased for business or promotional use. For information on bulk
purchases please contact Macmillan Corporate and Premium Sales Department at
specialmarkets@macmillan.com

Library of Congress Cataloging-in-Publication Data
Bloomberg, Georgina.
Rein it in : an A circuit novel / by Georgina Bloomberg and Catherine Hapka.
pages cm
Summary: Only the best of the best qualify for Indoors, a series of fall horse shows.
And of course, Tommi, Kate, and Zara are the best. Still, it's not exactly convenient
that this show series starts up just as school is back in session.
ISBN 978-1-61963-102-1 (paperback) • ISBN 978-1-61963-103-8 (e-book)
[1. Horse shows—Fiction. 2. Horsemanship—Fiction. 3. Friendship—Fiction.
4. Wealth—Fiction.] I. Hapka, Cathy. II. Title.
PZ7.B62345Re 2013   [Fic]—dc23   2013008988

Book design by Regina Flath
Typeset by Westchester Book Composition
Printed and bound in the U.S.A. by Thomson-Shore Inc., Dexter, Michigan
2 4 6 8 10 9 7 5 3 1

All papers used by Bloomsbury Publishing, Inc., are natural, recyclable products
made from wood grown in well-managed forests. The manufacturing processes
conform to the environmental regulations of the country of origin.

ONE

Zara woke with a start when the bell rang, signaling the end of her US History class. The geeky guy who sat across the aisle was just closing his notebook.

"Hey, uh . . ." Zara fished for his name. She was pretty sure he'd introduced himself on the first day of school, but that was weeks ago, and they'd barely spoken since. "Um, dude. Homework?"

"Read chapters seven and eight, answer the discussion questions at the end of each chapter," the guy said without looking at her.

"Thanks." Zara sighed, shooting the teacher an irritated look. So far Drummond was okay as schools went. Cool old building, decent food in the cafeteria, enough weirdos among the student body to keep things interesting. The downside? Way too much homework.

Zara stuffed her history book in her leather tote and slung the bag over her shoulder. Yawning, she headed for the door.

The halls were pandemonium. A pair of matching blond

girls emerged from the classroom across the way and zeroed in on Zara. She was pretty sure they were juniors, since they were both in her English class.

"Hi, Zara," the perkier of the two said. "How's it going?"

"It's going." Zara forced a smile. "You know, whatever."

Zara didn't even try to remember their names. She didn't need to—she knew their type. On Zara's first day, when they'd thought she was just another new girl, they totally ignored her. As soon as they'd found out who her parents were, that had changed. Even here, where most of the students came from serious Manhattan money, a rock star's kid was still at least a little bit of a novelty. Or maybe it was the movie star mom that had impressed them—now that she thought about it, Zara vaguely recalled one of the girls saying something about wanting to be an actress. Either way, Zara was over it.

Spotting a familiar face over near the stairwell, Zara spit out a quick "Gotta go" and took off. "Tommi!" she called. "Hey, wait up."

Tommi glanced back and smiled. Zara had to admit it had been nice having a friend at Drummond from the start. She wasn't the shy type—far from it—but starting a new school wasn't her favorite thing in the world.

Not that she would have guessed a few months ago that she and Tommi Aaronson would ever be friends. The two of them hadn't exactly hit it off when they'd first met at the stable where they both kept their horses. But eventually the two of them had found common ground—not only in riding, but also in coming from families where the judges at the shows weren't the only ones analyzing your every move. Zara still wasn't sure exactly what Tommi's father did—something

Wall-Streety—but she and everyone else in New York knew that Richard Aaronson's net worth was about the same as that of a small European nation. That made people jump to a lot of conclusions about what Tommi was like, and Zara definitely knew how that felt. Half the pictures in her baby album were clipped out of the tabloids.

It wasn't until Zara got closer that she noticed Tommi was walking with a couple of her senior friends. Crap. That kid everyone called Duckface seemed okay, but Court had been on Zara's nerves since the day they'd met. The girl was seriously overcaffeinated. Zara had no clue what Tommi saw in her.

"What's up?" Tommi asked when Zara reached them.

"Not much." Zara tossed a vague wave in the direction of Tommi's friends. "You get that text from Joy this morning?"

Tommi nodded, hoisting her hobo bag higher on her shoulder. "Group lesson this afternoon. Last one before the horses leave for the show. Jamie expects everyone to be there, no exceptions. Need a ride?"

"Sure, thanks."

"Ugh." Duckface rolled his eyes dramatically at Court. "They're talking horses. Come on, babycakes, let's get out of here before they start comparing their ponies' poop again."

Tommi grinned. "Hey, we only did that once."

"Yeah, but it was at *lunch*." Court grabbed Duckface by the arm. "Later, Tommi. Bye, Zara."

"See you." Zara was glad to see them go. She fell into step beside Tommi. "You must be psyched to leave for the show. Congrats again on qualifying for, like, everything at Indoors."

Tommi shrugged. "What can I say? I'm lucky to have talented horses. And even luckier that all of them stayed sound all season." She knocked lightly on the wooden banister of the stairwell.

She was playing modest, but Zara knew better. Most people at Drummond probably had no clue what a big deal it was to compete at the series of superprestigious fall horse shows collectively known on the A circuit as Indoors, due to their locations in indoor arenas. But Zara knew. She also knew it took more than luck to qualify with multiple horses in multiple divisions like Tommi had done. Again, most of Zara and Tommi's schoolmates probably couldn't differentiate among hunters, jumpers, and equitation if their lives depended on it. To them, it was all just horses jumping over stuff. But the three divisions required different skills. It took a lot of hard work to master even one, let alone all three. Zara knew that from experience.

"I think Jamie's pissed that Ellie and I didn't qualify for as much as he hoped we would," she said. "He probably regrets selling a superstar mare like that to a spaz like me."

She was only half kidding. Their trainer, Jamie Vos, was definitely a perfectionist. Zara? Not so much.

Tommi shot her a look. "Doubtful. Jamie doesn't believe in regrets. Besides, he knows you two are still getting to know each other. And you qualified for the Small Juniors at Harrisburg, right?"

"Barely. But hey, at least Ellie and I will get to show our stuff at Capital Challenge next week, too. Hooray for not needing to qualify to go to that one, right?" Zara picked at a cuticle as she walked. "Plus Keeper and I qualified for some jumper stuff, so . . ."

She let her voice trail off as she noticed a tiny redhead

careening toward them. "Zara, I just heard!" the girl said breathlessly, skidding to a stop right in front of Zara and peering into her face. "Is it true?"

Zara took a step back. "Is what true?"

The girl didn't seem to hear the question. "You must be devastated," she said, shaking her head. "I can't believe—"

"Girls!" a sharp voice interrupted. "Shouldn't you all be on your way to class right now?"

Zara didn't have to turn around to recognize that voice. It belonged to her algebra teacher, Ms. Rivera. Better known to most of the student body as the Dragon Lady of Drummond.

The redhead let out a squeak and scooted away, with a whispered "Bye, Zara!"

"We're going, too, Ms. Rivera," Tommi said. "Sorry."

Zara followed as Tommi hurried up the stairs. "Who was that girl?" Zara asked.

"She's a sophomore," Tommi said. "Her name's Becky, I think. What was she talking about?"

"Got me." Zara glanced over her shoulder, even though the younger girl was long gone. "Probably the latest not-so-hot gossip from our not-so-favorite blog."

Tommi shrugged. "Probably. I can't believe nobody's figured out who's writing that thing yet."

"Preach it." Zara grimaced as she thought about the blog, HorseShowSecrets. It had appeared out of nowhere late that summer, featuring gossip about riders at all the top East Coast barns, including Jamie's. Zara was used to ignoring her own press, but this was different. Whoever was writing the blog was obviously an A circuit insider, which somehow seemed worse than just another story by some lame-ass Hollywood stringer.

Pulling her smartphone out of her bag, Zara started typing in the address as she walked. Okay, so she hated to encourage the stupid blog by giving it more hits. But that sophomore had been worked up enough to make Zara think she'd better find out what the blogger was saying this time.

"Heads up," Tommi hissed.

Too late. Zara looked up to see her Spanish teacher, Mr. Wallace, striding toward her.

"What's the emergency, Senorita Trask?" he boomed out in his loud voice. "Feel a heart attack coming on? Hair on fire? What? Because I *know* you're aware of the school rules regarding cell phones."

"Um, do bad cramps count as an emergency?" Zara smiled weakly.

The teacher held out his hand. Zara sighed, clicked off the power on her phone, and handed it over.

"You can pick this up at the office after the final bell." Mr. Wallace nodded at her, then glanced at Tommi. "Now get to class before I have to give you both a demerit."

As the teacher strode off, Tommi shot Zara a sympathetic look. "I can't even count how many times I've had my phone confiscated."

"Yeah," Zara muttered. "This place needs to move out of the eighteenth century and realize we need our phones."

They'd reached Zara's next class by then, and Tommi paused outside the door. "Guess you'll have to wait to find out the latest."

"I won't hold my breath." Zara rolled her eyes. "Probably just another snotty thing about how I didn't manage to qualify the fanciest hunter on the planet for anything."

Tommi smiled. "Meet you at out front after school?"

"I'll be there."

Kate stuffed her books into her well-worn backpack as slowly as she could, keeping one eye on her chemistry teacher. The bell had just rung to release the class to lunch, and most of the other students weren't wasting any time stampeding out of the room. But Kate wasn't thinking about lunch. She needed to talk to Mr. Barron, and that was enough to make anyone feel queasy.

The teacher was talking to one of Kate's classmates, his brows drawn together in a frown that made him look even sterner than usual. Kate picked up her backpack and took a few tentative steps toward the front of the room.

"Look out!"

"Oof." Kate lurched forward as she felt a sharp elbow connect squarely with her lower back. As she grabbed at the nearest chair to stop herself from falling, she lost her grip on her backpack. It went flying, bouncing off the edge of a desk and spilling books, papers, and pens everywhere.

Her face flaming, Kate immediately bent and started gathering up her stuff. She didn't have to hear the familiar snicker to know that the collision had been no accident.

"You should watch where you're going, Katie."

Nat's voice was cold and harsh. Kate had always known that Nat had a mean streak, but somehow she'd managed to ignore it—mostly, anyway—all those years they were friends.

"Yeah. Watch where you're going, moron." Nat's latest boyfriend, a loser named Cody, kicked Kate's history book under a desk. Then he threw an arm around Nat's shoulders. "Let's go, babe. It stinks around here."

"You're telling me." Nat tossed her head and headed for the door.

Kate felt tears welling up in her eyes, though she gritted her teeth to stop them from escaping. She knew she shouldn't let Nat's garbage get to her. After weeks of dealing with her attitude, she should be used to it. But she wasn't. It still hurt—every time.

"You need help?"

Kate glanced up. A guy she barely knew named Jon was kneeling down to grab a tube of ChapStick that had rolled under a desk. "Oh," Kate said. "Um, thanks. I've got it."

"Here." Jon handed over the lip balm. Then he shot a look at Nat and Cody, who were just disappearing into the hallway. "What was that all about, anyway? I thought you and Nat were friends."

"I guess," Kate mumbled, hoping he wouldn't ask any more questions. It hurt even to think about her relationship with Nat, let alone try to explain it to someone who didn't know the story. What normal person would believe a lifelong friendship had ended over a horse? Kate could hardly believe it herself—especially since horses were what had brought her and Nat together, back in the days when they both rode at Happy Acres, a local lesson barn.

Things had started to change between Kate and Nat two and a half years ago, when Kate had left to become a working student at Pelham Lane, the fanciest barn in the area. Nat had never even heard of Jamie Vos, and didn't get why Kate would ditch her old barn and her old friends for some snooty show stable where she had to work twice as hard for half as much riding time.

Still, they'd managed to get through it and remain friends. Until last summer . . .

"Here."

Kate blinked, snapping out of her thoughts. Jon was handing over her history book.

"Um, thanks." Kate quickly stuffed the book into her bag. She was surprised someone like Jon had even noticed that she and Nat had been friends, since he'd been new in school last year. At least, she was pretty sure he was new. It was hard to keep track of everyone at their enormous suburban public school, especially since Kate's mind was usually at the barn even when the rest of her wasn't.

"Miss Nilsen, Mr. Friedman?" Mr. Barron had finished with the other student. Now he was staring at Kate and Jon. "May I help you with something?"

Kate gulped and stepped forward. "I—I wanted to ask you about homework for next week?" she said. "I'm going to be away, and you said I should check back today. . . ."

"Oh right. A horseback riding vacation or something, was it?" The teacher's voice was vaguely disapproving.

"The Capital Challenge Horse Show," Kate said, clutching her bookbag to her stomach. "It's in Maryland. I'll be working there all week."

"I see." Mr. Barron rustled through the papers on his desk. "Well, I have to admit I'm skeptical of this plan, Miss Nilsen. Your grades so far this semester haven't been stellar, to say the least."

Kate swallowed hard. "I know. But I've been studying like crazy lately, I swear. And I got a B-plus on the last quiz."

"Yes." The teacher studied her for a moment. "Well, I suppose we'll give it a try. I've put together a packet for you, and I'll expect all the assigned work completed and turned in as soon as you return. And of course you'll need to work extra hard in the weeks after you get back to show me that it was worth my effort to do this."

Kate gulped, almost afraid to remind him of the rest. "Uh, I'll be gone for some of those later weeks, too. There are three more shows right after this one, and I'm supposed to work at all of them."

The teacher's eyes narrowed. "I see."

Kate held her breath. For the past two years, she'd watched Jamie and the others head off to Indoors and wished she could go too. This was the first year Jamie had agreed to allow it— but only if she promised to keep up with her schoolwork. That had seemed like an easy promise to make at the time, but the reality was turning out to be trickier than Kate had expected.

"It's no big deal," she blurted out, feeling her cheeks go pink. "I mean, I know people from this school don't usually do this. But other riders my age go to Indoors every year, and do the Florida circuit in the winter, too. I mean, most of them go to private schools, where they're used to students doing stuff like that, but . . ."

She let her voice trail off. Judging by the deepening frown on the teacher's face, her explanations weren't helping.

"Interesting, but irrelevant," Mr. Barron said. "I don't care what other students do. I'm only concerned with *my* students. Just how much school will you be missing, exactly?"

"Um, I'm not sure yet," Kate hedged. "After Cap Challenge I'll be back for a couple of days, then we leave for Harrisburg—um, that's the Pennsylvania National Horse Show—on Wednesday afternoon. Then another break before the Washington International down in DC, and then last is the National in Kentucky."

The teacher's expression soured more with each show Kate listed. "I'm afraid when you first mentioned this to me, Miss Nilsen, I didn't fully understand the scope of your commitment," he said. "I think I'd better discuss this with your parents before we go any further. When would be the best time to call them?"

"What?" Panic squeezed Kate's throat, making it hard to breathe. "Um, are you sure that's necessary? They're really busy right now, and they already signed the permission slip to let me miss school next week—it's filed in the main office."

She tried not to let her desperation show. Mr. Barron couldn't call her parents—well, her father, really, since her mother never answered the phone anymore. A disapproving comment from a teacher might be all it took to make her parents change their minds, since they were barely on board with the whole Indoors thing as it was. Technically, the only show they'd actually agreed to let her attend so far was Capital Challenge. They'd left the others open to discussion once they saw how the first one went. Not that Kate had told Jamie that . . .

Mr. Barron was still frowning as he glanced at his watch. "Fine. But I want to go on record as thinking this isn't the best idea for your academic well-being, Miss Nilsen. You'll need to prove me wrong."

"Okay," Kate said weakly. "Thanks."

She took the bulging manila envelope he handed her, trying not to notice how heavy it was. Only then did she notice Jon hanging out by the door, waiting for her.

"What was that all about?" he asked as they emerged into the hall, which had emptied out almost completely as everyone headed to lunch. "You're going to a horse show?"

"Not just a horse show." Kate paused to stuff the manila envelope into her bag. "It's one of the biggest shows of the year. People come from all over the country for it."

"Oh. Like the Kentucky Derby or something?"

Kate swallowed a sigh. Why did it seem as if the general public had never heard of any horse sport other than racing?

"Yeah," she said. "Something like that, I guess."

Just then her cell phone buzzed. She fished it out and found a text from Fitz.

Bored to death in French right now. Why can't we all just speak the same language? Wish u were here to tickle my feet & wake me up. Ooh la la!

Kate couldn't help smiling. Sometimes she still got a weird, sort of unreal feeling when Fitz looked at her or kissed her or even sent her a text. The feeling that this had to be a dream or a joke, because Fitz Hall—wealthy, witty, gorgeous Fitz Hall—couldn't possibly be her boyfriend. But those moments were getting less frequent, replaced by the more comfortable feeling that maybe Fitz really did care about her. That maybe the two of them did have something special, like he'd told her from the beginning. That they were right for each other despite their very different backgrounds.

"Anything important?" Jon asked.

Kate quickly stuck the phone back in her bag. "Just a text from a friend."

But the smile stuck with her all the way to her locker. So many things were difficult these days—Nat, her family, school. Even her job at the barn stressed her out.

Then there was Fitz. Sweet, silly, sexy Fitz, who somehow hadn't become bored with her yet. Who still seemed just as smitten with her as ever, despite his playboy rep. Who was sometimes the only one who could make her smile when things started getting to her.

At least she still had one thing that was easy.

TWO

———   ———   ———   ———   ———

It was getting dark by the time Tommi pulled her BMW into one of the last open spots in Pelham Lane's gravel parking area.

"Looks like it's going to be crowded in the indoor today." Zara sounded cranky as she unclicked her seat belt.

Tommi knew how she felt. Now that school had started and it was getting dark earlier, the juniors and working adults were mostly stuck riding in the indoor ring during the week. The indoor was one of the largest in Westchester County, but even so, with that many riders it could feel awfully cramped.

"We'd better get inside." Tommi checked her watch. They'd gotten stuck behind an accident on the Triborough Bridge, which had delayed them for almost forty-five minutes. "Everyone else is probably here already."

They headed into the big main barn, which was brightly lit and full of activity. Max, one of the grooms, was hustling by with a wheelbarrow full of fresh shavings. An adult rider was buckling her helmet while talking on her cell phone. An alert-looking Jack Russell terrier trotted past with a leather jumping boot in his mouth.

A second later Joy, the barn's assistant trainer, raced into view. "Whiskey, get back here!" she exclaimed.

Tommi darted forward and grabbed the dog's pink rhinestone-studded collar. "Stop, thief," she said with a grin.

"Thanks, Tommi." Joy wrestled the boot out of the dog's mouth, then straightened up and smiled. "Hi, Zara. You guys better get ready—Jamie's in a hurry tonight."

Tommi released Whiskey's collar. The rowdy little dog belonged to Summer Campbell, another junior rider, and Tommi knew it was pointless to try to find her and convince her to keep him on a leash like she was supposed to. Somehow, Summer never seemed to believe the barn rules applied to her.

"Of course Jamie is frantic," Tommi told Joy with a smile. "We leave for the show tomorrow."

Joy chuckled. "You know him so well." Suddenly her smile faded. "Excuse me—I just remembered something."

She raced off down the main aisle toward the center section of the barn, where the office, tack room, restrooms, and various storage spaces were located. "Does she ever stop moving?" Zara wondered, watching her go.

Tommi shrugged. "Maybe when she's asleep. Come on, I'll walk you to Keeper's stall—it's right on my way."

As they headed deeper into the barn, another junior rider, Marissa, rounded the corner of the aisle. She was leading a kind-eyed bay gelding decked out in a Baker stable sheet.

"Zara!" Marissa exclaimed. "Oh wow, I wasn't sure you'd show tonight. You know—because of the news?"

For a second Tommi wasn't sure what she was talking about.

Then she remembered that odd encounter at school earlier that day. "Oh right. Did you ever figure out what the latest gossip is all about?" she asked Zara.

"No. I was rushing to meet you after school and forgot to get my phone back from the office." Zara raised an eyebrow at Marissa. "Care to fill me in?"

Marissa's already-round brown eyes widened. "You mean you haven't heard?" She pulled an iPhone out of the pocket of her Tailored Sportsmans and worked it with one hand while her horse nosed at her pocket, looking for treats. "Here," she said after a moment, shoving the phone toward Zara.

Tommi didn't really care about the latest stupid rumor and was about to move on to her horse's stall. But Zara's quick intake of breath stopped her.

"What?" Tommi asked.

Zara's full lips had all but disappeared into a thin, grim line. "See for yourself," she said, tossing Marissa's phone in Tommi's direction.

Tommi caught it and scanned the blog entry.

Can it be? Pelham Lane junior Zara Trask has become a fixture at the East Coast shows since her famous father, Zac Trask, moved the family from LA to NYC. Now rumor has it that Zac might be getting more involved with Zara's riding . . . and maybe even with one of her fellow juniors!

"So is it true?" Marissa tugged on the reins to stop her horse from wandering past her to check out the hay flakes stacked in a wheelbarrow nearby. "Because everyone is already trying to figure out who it could be." She giggled. "It's not me, I swear!"

Tommi almost rolled her eyes. Marissa was cute enough, with her dimpled smile and curly dark hair, but somehow Tommi couldn't see an international superstar like Zac Trask even noticing her, let along risking scandal to have an illicit affair with her.

"*So* not true," Zara snapped. "Duh! When was the last time you even saw my dad around this place? Let me think—it was the day before *never!*"

"Yeah. I figured it was just a rumor." Marissa actually sounded disappointed. Tommi wasn't surprised. The girl lived for gossip. "Anyway, I'm sure nobody really believes it."

"Whatever." Zara frowned and turned away. "Better go get ready."

She stalked off down the aisle. Tommi could tell she was annoyed, but she'd get over it. Her whole life took place in the public eye, pretty much. And this was far from the worst thing that had ever been written about her or her parents. For a moment, it actually made Tommi feel grateful for her own family situation. Okay, so everyone knew her last name, and it was annoying to know that a lot of people would always believe she'd bought her success in the show ring instead of working for it. But at least her father wasn't the type of guy who got accused of crazy scandals. Or *any* scandals, for that matter. Even thinking about it made Tommi smile, picturing him puttering around the house in his half-moon glasses and scuffed suede slippers, with a copy of the *Wall Street Journal* dragging along losing pages behind him.

"I should get going, too," she told Marissa. "See you in the ring."

Soon she was leading her equitation horse, a massive

warmblood gelding named Orion, into a grooming stall. A lanky, restless bay Thoroughbred was already cross-tied in the next bay over. His owner, Dani, was humming as she groomed him.

"How's the leg?" Tommi asked as she clipped the ties to Orion's halter.

Dani glanced over, then grinned and did a funny little jig step. "Good as new," she said, smacking herself on the thigh. "Not that Jamie believes it. He totally banished me from riding at Cap Challenge—says it's too soon."

"He's just being cautious, like always." Tommi grabbed a brush out of her grooming kit. "I think it really freaked him out when you got hurt."

She still winced a bit herself every time she thought about that lesson. Dani had been lucky to get away with just a broken leg when her horse had tossed her into the ring's wooden fence. The cast had come off a little over a week ago, and Dani had needed every ounce of her outgoing, optimistic personality to convince Jamie she was ready to ride at the upcoming indoor shows—some of them, at least.

Just then Summer clattered into view, dragging her horse along behind her. "Am I late?" she asked. "My mom's stupid business meeting ran like a million hours overtime. Then when I got here, I had to spend another million hours searching for my bridle. Why can't people just leave stuff where it's supposed to be?"

Tommi traded a quick, amused look with Dani. Pelham Lane was the most organized place imaginable, with a place for everything and everything in its place. Summer, on the other hand, was notorious for leaving her things strewn around the barn and expecting the staff to put them all away for her.

"You'll be fine if you hurry," Tommi told Summer.

Dani nodded. "I'm not sure Fitz is even here yet."

"Oh. Good." Summer led her horse into a grooming stall. "So what are you guys talking about?"

"Just my leg," Dani said. "I was saying Jamie's still acting like it'll break again if anyone looks at me cross-eyed. He convinced my parents to lock me in my room until after Cap Challenge." She rolled her eyes dramatically.

"You're still going to Harrisburg though, right?" Summer asked. "You should totally write in to that blog and tell them that. Because everyone's probably wondering since that post last week."

"What post?" Tommi asked.

"Didn't you see it? You must be, like, the only person on the circuit who didn't." Summer fiddled with her horse's halter. "It said all this stuff about how Dani was, like, battling with Jamie over whether he'd allow her to ride at Indoors at all."

"Hmm." Suddenly Tommi was tired of hearing about the stupid blog. Time for a change of subject. Shifting her brush to her other hand, she glanced at Dani. "So you're definitely going to Harrisburg though, right? Did you qualify for either of the other shows, or wasn't there time what with the leg thing?"

"Luckily Red and I snagged enough points early." Dani grabbed a saddle pad and slung it over her horse's back, causing him to dance in place and snort. "We're in with room to spare at Washington, but just squeaked through over the cutoff for the National."

"Nice." Tommi tossed the brush back into her kit. Capital

Challenge or not, she knew Dani had to be pleased with her upcoming show schedule. Her horse was talented and scopey but could be challenging to ride, and the year before the pair hadn't racked up enough points to qualify for anything at Indoors.

"Hey, I forgot my girth," Summer said. "Watch my horse for a sec, okay?"

"Sure," Tommi said, though Summer was already rushing off without waiting for a response. Her horse had one hind leg cocked and appeared to be falling asleep in the cross-ties, so he wasn't likely to go anywhere.

Besides, it was practically a miracle that Summer was tacking up for the lesson herself instead of trying to finagle a groom into doing it for her. Jamie wanted his program to turn out horsemen, not just riders, which meant he liked the serious juniors to do as much of their own horse care as their skills and schedules allowed. And right before a show that preference became a rule, at least when it came to grooming and tacking up, since the grooms had more than enough to do without stopping to prepare a horse for a junior who was feeling lazy. Not that Summer usually paid attention to that sort of thing. Tommi guessed that the trainer must have had another talk with her.

Dani peered over the divider. "Hey, I heard Jamie saying Legs is going to be at Cap Challenge with his new owner," she said. "That's cool, right?"

"Definitely." Tommi kept her voice casual. Thinking about Legs, the horse she'd sold right before school started, filled her with mixed emotions. He was meant to be the first step in a new business venture she hoped might eventually turn into a career in buying, training, and reselling show horses. She'd convinced her father to fund part of Legs's purchase, with the idea that if the first sale was a success, he would continue to help her build the business. Tommi was proud of herself for bringing Legs along and selling him so quickly, and thrilled that his new owner seemed to be doing so well with him.

On the other hand, thinking about Legs reminded her that weeks had passed and she hadn't moved forward with her plans. At first she hadn't worried about it, figuring she needed a break to focus on starting her senior year at school and figuring out her schedule for Indoors.

But now she was ready for the next step, and despite their deal, her father seemed to be dragging his heels. Every time Tommi mentioned wanting to start looking at prospects, he changed the subject—usually by reminding her she needed to start thinking about college applications and campus visits.

"Are you okay?"

Tommi blinked, realizing she was staring into space. She glanced at Dani and smiled.

"Yeah," she said. "Just thinking about how to convince my dad it's time for me to pick up another project horse."

Dani flicked a speck of hay off her horse's glossy coat. "He doesn't want you to get another one?"

"No, it's not that." Tommi hesitated, trying to figure out how to explain her father to someone who didn't really know him. "I'm sure he'll be convinced when I find the right horse."

She bit her lip, turning away and fiddling with Orion's mane so Dani couldn't see how aggravated she was. She hated that her new business was stalled just when it should be taking off. But what could she do? If she pushed too hard, her father was likely to just say no to the whole plan.

"I'm back!" Summer sang out, skipping into the grooming aisle with Whiskey at her heels. "And we'd better hurry. Marissa's already heading for the indoor."

"Hey, big boy," Kate murmured, letting herself into the stall where a tall, attractive chestnut gelding was nibbling at his hay. "How's it going? Bet you're wondering what all the extra commotion is around here. Then again, I guess you were used to lots of commotion at the racetrack, huh?"

She smiled as the horse nuzzled her. Flame had only been at Pelham Lane since late summer, but Kate already had trouble imagining the place without him.

Her smile faded slightly as her mind jumped back to her encounter with Nat earlier. Was it any wonder Nat was still holding a grudge? She thought Kate had stolen Flame from her.

Okay, so that wasn't technically true. Nat had never owned Flame, and Fitz had bought him from the owners of Happy Acres fair and square.

Still. If Nat hadn't invited Kate to come watch her ride Flame in that schooling show over the summer, and if Kate hadn't spent half the time there gushing about what a diamond in the rough the horse was, then Fitz never would have come up with the crazy idea to buy him and get Kate to help turn him into a show hunter. Once Kate realized how that must have made Nat feel, she'd tried to apologize to her— to explain how it had happened and ask what she could do to make it up to her. But Nat hadn't even let her finish before cutting her off and slamming the door in her face. Literally and otherwise.

Kate picked a shaving out of Flame's silky mane, trying not to think about Nat. "Wish I could give you a nice grooming, boy. But there's so much to do . . ." She sighed as she checked her watch. It was time to get tacked up, or she'd be late for the lesson.

For a moment she was tempted to skip it. After all, she wouldn't be competing at the big shows like the others. Not really. Oh, sure, she'd probably end up catch-riding a few for Jamie, maybe taking something in the hack for someone with multiple mounts or doing a warm-up class here and there.

And usually that was fine. But this was Indoors. Just once, Kate wished she could find out what it felt like to step into the big ring for real. . . .

"Kate! There you are," Joy's cheerful voice broke into Kate's thoughts. The assistant trainer paused outside Flame's stall, a saddle balanced on her hip. "The other juniors are almost ready for the lesson—even a certain handsome young gentleman who tends to be late." She winked and smiled. "You'd better get a move on."

Kate let herself out of the stall. "Yeah, about that. Since the others will be practicing for the show, I was thinking I might skip it today. They won't miss me, and I've got a ton to do—the guys could use more help packing up the trailers, and—"

"Not so fast." Joy held up a hand to stop her. "You earned this lesson with all that work you've been doing, remember? Jamie wouldn't want you to skip it."

"But I don't need the practice, since I'm not riding in any of the big classes at Cap Challenge."

"Okay. But Jamie's counting on you to keep Fable in shape and improving, remember? And you'll be away for over a week. He needs this ride, even if you don't."

"Oh. Yeah, I guess." Kate hadn't thought about it that way. Fabelhaften, better known as Fable, was at Pelham Lane to be sold for his wealthy owners, who'd moved to Europe in the spring. The big, athletic gray Hanoverian had already dabbled in a couple of other disciplines, most recently the hunters, but Jamie believed his true talents lay in the equitation ring. He'd asked Kate to take over the ride and campaign Fable in the competitive Big Eq classes, where the pair had held their own against Tommi, Fitz, and other top juniors from all over the zone.

"Besides"—Joy leaned closer and winked—"maybe you didn't have enough time to qualify for the Big Eq finals *this* year. But there's always next year, right? And if you and Fable keep on the way you're going . . ." She waggled her eyebrows meaningfully.

Kate smiled, grateful as always for the assistant trainer's positive outlook. "Okay," she said. "I guess I'll—"

"Excuse me." Joy's face suddenly went pale. She dumped the saddle onto the floor, leaning it up against the wall. "I'll be back for this later. I just remembered something else I have to do. Have a good lesson."

"Thanks," Kate said, though Joy was already halfway down the aisle at a brisk jog.

"What was that all about?" a voice said behind Kate.

Turning, Kate saw Dani walking toward her, leading her tacked-up jumper. Tommi was right behind her with her eq horse.

"Hi," Kate greeted them. "Wow, I'm even farther behind than I thought."

"Is Joy sick or something?" Dani asked.

"I don't think so." Kate quickly latched Flame's stall shut and gave the horse one last pat. "Why?"

Dani shrugged. "She's been acting kind of weird lately. Like, distracted and rushing off randomly and stuff. Everyone's noticed."

Tommi stopped her horse beside Dani's. "She's probably just stressed out getting ready for Indoors like the rest of us. I bet she'll be thrilled to see the trailers pull out of here tomorrow so she can relax."

"Yeah." Dani laughed. "If you can call running the whole place almost single-handedly while we're gone *relaxing*."

Kate glanced off in the direction the assistant trainer had gone, hoping that Joy was okay. In any case, she didn't have time to worry about it just then.

"Listen, tell Jamie I'm on my way, okay?" she called to Tommi and Dani as she took off toward Fable's stall.

Ten minutes later, Kate was breathless and had a smudge of green horse slobber across her shirt as she led Fable to the mounting block right outside the gate of the indoor ring. Fitz spotted her immediately and rode over.

"You made it," he called out as she swung into the saddle. "Jamie's not here yet."

"Really?" Kate picked up her reins as Fable took a few quick steps away from the block. Once she got the big gray settled, she glanced around. Tommi was trotting in circles at one end of the ring. Zara was trying to convince her mare to trot instead of jigging sideways toward Summer's horse, which was stopped in the center of the ring while Summer fiddled with her stirrups. Marissa and Dani were chatting as they walked their horses around side by side on the buckle.

Most of the riders glanced over as Kate rode into the ring. "Oh, it's you," Summer said. "I thought it was Jamie."

"Where *is* he, anyway?" Marissa glanced at her watch. "He's usually Mr. Prompt."

"No kidding," Zara agreed. "He yelled at me for, like, half an hour last week because I was thirty seconds late."

Kate suspected she was exaggerating, but probably not by much. "Maybe he forgot about our lesson," she suggested. "He's really busy today."

"In that case, we might as well start without him." Fitz halted his horse in the center of the ring and raised one hand in a fist. "You must all obey me, the almighty self-appointed trainer!"

Tommi rolled her eyes. "Yeah, right."

But Dani giggled. "Okay, almighty one," she said. "What do you want us to do?"

"We need to warm up these lazy beasts." Fitz tapped his own horse lightly on the neck with his crop. "Working trot on the rail, everyone. No dawdling—make them move!"

Kate traded a look with Tommi. Tommi shrugged. "Sounds like what Jamie would say. Guess we might as well humor him for now."

For the next few minutes, Fitz directed the class through their warm-up. Just as Kate was wondering if Jamie really had forgotten about them, the trainer finally appeared in the doorway.

"It's about time, young man!" Fitz chided. "Where were—oh, sorry. Um, just kidding."

Kate looked over again and saw the reason Fitz had backed off. Two people were coming into the indoor behind the trainer—a man and woman in their thirties or early forties. Both of them were casually dressed in jeans and loafers, but they had a certain look Kate had learned to recognize since coming to Pelham Lane—the look of money. Probably lots of it.

"Sorry I'm late, everyone." Jamie shot a warning look at Fitz, then glanced around at the others. "Come on over here, people. I'd like you to meet Cari and Mike Langley. Fable's owners."

For a second Kate thought she'd heard him wrong. True, she knew Fable had owners somewhere out there, but she'd never even seen them.

"Whoa," Marissa whispered just loudly enough for Kate to hear. "I thought they moved to Sweden or somewhere."

"I think it was Switzerland," Tommi murmured.

Kate didn't say anything. Suddenly she was all too aware of that smudge on her shirt, the wisps of blond hair escaping from under her helmet, the pale green manure stain she hadn't had time to rub completely out of Fable's gray coat.

"Hi, everyone!" Mrs. Langley lifted a hand and smiled. "Sorry to interrupt your lesson. We were back in New York for a few days and decided to pop in and see how Fabelhaften is doing. I miss the big lug!"

Meanwhile her husband was peering at Fable. "He's looking terrific, Jamie. Your program obviously agrees with him."

"I hope so." Jamie waved Kate over. "I want you to meet the talented young rider I was telling you about. She's been doing a fantastic job with him. Come here and say hello, Kate."

"Hi," Kate halted by the rail near the couple. "Um, thanks for letting me ride Fable and show him and everything."

"No, thank *you*, Kate," Mr. Langley said. "We hear you're turning the horse into a superstar of the Big Eq ring."

"That's right," Jamie put in. "As I mentioned to you on the phone last week, they unfortunately didn't have quite enough time to qualify for finals this year. But I'm expecting big things from them next season."

"Wonderful." Mrs. Langley stroked Fable's nose as the gelding stretched his head toward her. "We appreciate all your hard work, Kate. But wait—didn't Jamie say you're all leaving for the Capital Challenge tomorrow? If Fable's not going, shouldn't you be riding one of your other horses to get ready?"

"Good point." Mr. Langley chuckled and clapped Fable on the neck. "We're not in *that* much of a hurry to get this fella sold."

Kate opened her mouth, but no sound came out. Behind her, she heard a soft snort and guessed that Summer was rolling her eyes at the ridiculous thought that anyone could mistake Kate for one of them—one of the privileged juniors with at least one nice horse of her own, if not several.

"Kate and I thought Fable would benefit from the exercises we'll be doing in today's lesson," Jamie put in smoothly. "Which reminds me, we'd better get started. You're welcome to watch from the viewing lounge."

As the couple hurried off, Kate immediately put Fable back to work, trotting him in a big, loopy circle without meeting any of her fellow juniors' eyes. She already knew what she would find there. The amusement and disdain in Summer's wouldn't bother her much.

But she wasn't sure she could handle the sympathy, concern, or pity she was sure to see in the others.

THREE

A shiver ran through Tommi's entire body as she heard the show announcer say her number. She felt as if she hadn't stopped moving since arriving at the Capital Challenge show-grounds a couple of days ago, but all of a sudden it was as if everything had gone still. As if the entire place was holding its breath, waiting for her to begin her first equitation round.

"Let's do this, buddy," she whispered.

Orion's left ear flicked back toward her. The other was still pricked toward the ring in front of them. The experienced eq horse had been to all the finals before with his previous owner, and to this particular show with Tommi the year before. Still, he felt tense under her as he took in the spooky indoor arena. Tommi was tense, too. The North American Junior Equitation Championships wasn't the most prestigious of the fall finals, but it was a pretty big deal.

Tommi clucked and sent Orion into the ring at a trot, then picked up a canter. As soon as he was moving, the horse relaxed, as Tommi had known he would. She glanced toward the first jump on the course, a substantial but inviting brick wall with white rails.

Orion sailed over it easily, pricking his ears in search of the next one. His canter felt a little sluggish, so Tommi gave him a nudge with her calves and then steered around the turn. Short approach to a good-sized oxer. Once again the horse cleared it out of stride.

The next two jumps went just as well, though Tommi still found herself having to use more leg than usual. She wasn't too worried about it, though. Horses reacted in different ways to a big class like this one. Most got amped and wanted to go faster than usual, but today Orion seemed to be slowing down, maybe trying to get a better look at the heavily deco- rated fences. As long as he responded promptly to her leg, Tommi wasn't concerned.

They landed smoothly out of a tricky combination and headed for the fifth fence, another oxer. It came off a rather tight turn, which didn't worry Tommi much. For a large horse, Orion was surprisingly agile.

This time, though, he stumbled badly as they rounded the turn, flinging Tommi forward in the saddle. She recovered quickly, sitting up and back and pushing the horse forward. But Orion's metronome-like gait faltered for several strides, and despite Tommi's best attempts to adjust, they ended up long to the oxer. Orion flung himself over anyway, his hind legs clank- ing the back rail hard. The rail stayed up, but Tommi was sure that jump hadn't looked pretty.

She nudged the horse forward, urging him back into a

steady canter. With a few tiny adjustments, they reached the next fence perfectly, but Tommi knew it didn't matter. A bobble like that meant they were almost certainly out of contention for any kind of ribbon. Yes, equitation was judged on the rider's form and ability, not on the horse's scope or accuracy. Still, the judge could only judge what was in front of him or her, and Tommi's ride wasn't going to impress against riders who made it through the course smoothly. That was the way the cookie crumbled. Or the horse stumbled.

They finished the round without any other significant mistakes. Tommi heard whoops and applause from the Pelham Lane crew watching from the stands, and gritted her teeth as she forced a smile. At least the other eq finals were still to come, including the prestigious Medal at Harrisburg and the Maclay in Kentucky. She and Orion would have a chance to redeem themselves. For now, all she could do was accept what had happened and learn from it. Maybe if he'd been more forward; maybe if she'd supported him more with the reins through that tight turn . . .

Trying not to obsess over it, she patted Orion as they rode out of the ring. Jamie was waiting for her, along with one of Pelham Lane's grooms, Elliot.

"What happened?" Jamie asked.

Tommi shrugged and swung down from the saddle as Elliot reached for Orion's bridle. "Not sure," Tommi said. "He took a funny step or something. Just one of those things, I guess."

Jamie nodded, squinting toward the scoreboard. "Happens," he said. "We'll talk more later. I need to figure out where Fitz is—he's up soon."

Tommi ran up Orion's left stirrup as Elliot did the other

one. The groom was tall enough to glance at her over the horse's back.

"Sorry," he said. "The rest of the course looked good."

"Thanks." This time Tommi's smile came a little more easily. She unhooked her helmet strap. "We'll get 'em next time."

"That's the spirit." Elliot smiled back, then took the horse's reins. "I'll cool him out for you. Like Jamie said, Fitz is coming up soon—go cheer him on."

"Thanks." Fitz had been doing well in the eq all season, and Tommi didn't want to miss seeing him go.

She gave her horse one last pat, then headed in the general direction those cheers had come from. As she scanned the stands looking for her barnmates, she spotted another familiar face a few rows up from the rail. It belonged to an old friend from the circuit who had aged out of juniors the previous year.

"Taryn?" Tommi took the steps two at a time. "Is that you? What are you doing here?"

"Hi, Tommi." Taryn stood and came to meet her with a hug. She was tall and slim, with close-cropped dark hair and the kind of face that always looked happy even when she wasn't smiling. "I go to school right down the road from here, remember? So I decided to come by and spectate. You looked good out there, by the way. Too bad your horse tripped."

"Yeah, bad luck. Usually he's Mr. Sure-Footed." Tommi pulled off her riding gloves and set them on her knee as she took the seat beside Taryn's. "It's so good to see you! How's college?"

"Amazing." Taryn's brown eyes sparkled as she reached over and squeezed Tommi's arm. "You won't believe how much better it is than high school. In, like, *every* way."

"Hmm." Tommi glanced out at the ring, where a rider

from one of the best barns in New England had just cleared the first combination. "You must miss showing, though."

Taryn smiled. "Oh, I'm still showing."

"You are?" Tommi was surprised. She didn't remember seeing Taryn's name in the results for the Adult Amateur or Amateur Owner divisions at any show this year. "Where?"

"I'm riding for my college team." Taryn reached down and grabbed her purse from under her seat. She dug out her wallet and flipped it open to show Tommi a photo of herself on a horse, grinning at the camera. "See? That's me!" She laughed. "It's not exactly the A circuit, but it's a ton of fun."

"Your college team?" Tommi was vaguely aware that there was such a thing as a college riding team. But she'd never known anyone who was involved with one. Most of the older juniors she'd known from Pelham Lane—including her own older sister—had given up showing entirely when they went off to college.

"Yeah." Taryn tucked her wallet away again. "It's a blast. Seriously. You should give it a try—which schools are you applying to?"

"Um." Tommi felt a flash of irritation, though she did her best to hide it. It was bad enough to have her father breathing down her neck about college applications. Were her friends going to start now, too? "I haven't narrowed it down yet," she told Taryn.

Taryn started babbling about the best Web sites to check to find out which colleges had equestrian teams, but Tommi wasn't really listening. She'd just spotted Zara climbing up toward them.

"Hey," Zara said breathlessly when she reached their row.

"Looked like Orion forgot where his feet went for a sec there. Sorry."

"Thanks. Zara, this is Taryn. She used to ride with the Johnsons out on Long Island, but she aged out last year." Tommi glanced at Taryn. "And this is Zara. She rides with Jamie."

"Hi." Taryn stared at Zara with open curiosity. "You're Zac Trask's daughter, right?"

"Yeah." Zara's face tensed up. "That's me."

Tommi shot her a sympathetic look. It seemed as if everyone on the circuit had seen that blog post about Zac, and Tommi was sure a lot of people were giving Zara crap about it. Luckily, at that moment Taryn's eyes wandered past Zara, and she let out a gasp.

"Oh my gosh, there's Candace!" She stood and waved frantically at someone in another part of the arena. "Sorry, I've been looking for her all day—catch up later, Tommi?"

"Sure." Tommi lifted one hand in a little wave as Taryn grabbed her bag, climbed over Tommi's legs, and hurried off.

Zara slumped into the seat the other girl had vacated. "It's always nice to meet another fan," she said sarcastically.

"Taryn's okay." Tommi shrugged. "It's not like she's the only one who's a little curious about that blog thing."

"Whatever." Zara picked at a hangnail. "I'm just sick of hearing about it, is all. Here *and* at home."

Tommi raised an eyebrow. "So your dad heard about it, huh?"

She was a little surprised. Sure, HorseShowSecrets was a pretty big deal among the juniors on the A circuit. But as far as Tommi knew, even Jamie and Joy and most of the other adults at the barn had no idea it existed.

"Yeah. That post got picked up by some second-rate Hollywood gossip site," Zara said. "Then the other outlets started sniffing around, and, well . . ." She grimaced. "Let's just say I was glad to escape to the show."

"Wow." Tommi shook her head. "I hope it doesn't cause your dad too much trouble."

"Oh, Zac will get over it." Zara rolled her eyes. "This is why he pays all those managers and publicists and stuff, right? Anyway, all those middle-aged housewives who worship him probably think it's totally hot that he's allegedly hooking up with some underage twit." She pretended to gag.

Even though Zara sounded like her usual sarcastic self, Tommi sensed an undercurrent of real annoyance. "Wait," she said. "Your dad doesn't think *you* had anything to do with that rumor, does he?"

"I don't know. Maybe. Probably not." Zara fiddled with the zipper on her jacket. "I think the loft is just feeling a little crowded these days. For all of us."

Tommi nodded, recalling that both of Zara's parents had spent much of the summer and early fall in different countries—Zac on tour with his band in Europe, and Gina on a movie set in Vancouver. Tommi liked to think of herself as pretty independent, but even so, it was weird to imagine spending that much time on her own. Sure, her father and stepmother traveled some, but rarely for more than a couple of weeks at a time, and even then Tommi usually either flew to Florida to visit her mother or stayed with friends.

Just then a gasp went up from the crowd. Focusing on the ring again, Tommi saw that the current rider's horse, a big, wide-eyed gray, had just stopped at the second-to-last jump on course. It was backing up, shaking its head violently as the rider tried to regroup.

"Bummer," Tommi murmured.

"Hey, you should be happy—makes your round look better, right?" Zara shot Tommi a wicked grin.

Tommi laughed. "Thanks a lot, pal." Not wanting to stare at the poor girl in the ring, who was steering her still-agitated horse in a lopsided circle in front of the jump, she turned and glanced up at the stands. "So where's everybody else? Should we go find them?"

"Let's not and say we did." Zara was watching the action in the ring with interest. "They're a total snoozefest. Marissa is all panicked about some history paper she's supposed to turn in when we get back, and Summer just keeps forcing everybody to talk to her in French so she can practice her verb conjugations or whatever."

Tommi didn't answer. The girl on the gray had finally booted him over the last two jumps, and a male rider was entering the ring as she left. Even the boring eq uniform of navy jacket, dark tie, and Samshield helmet couldn't hide how good-looking he was.

"Who's *that*?" Tommi asked.

Zara turned to look. "Yeah, he's hot, isn't he?" she said. "I used to see him at some of the West Coast shows. Sadly never up close, if you know what I mean." She waggled her eyebrows. "His name starts with an S, I think—Steve, maybe? No, wait—Scott. I'm pretty sure that's it, Scott. I never paid much attention to the eq, but I think he used to win a lot."

"I can see why. He's good." Tommi watched as the guy sent his mount, a nervy jet-black horse, over the first fence. It didn't look easy, and Tommi suspected it wouldn't win many points with the judge, but she could tell it had taken some serious riding.

Zara shot her a sidelong look. "Careful, you don't want to drool all over your good jacket."

"Very funny." Tommi kept her eyes on the ring.

"How long has it been since you dumped Alex, anyway?" Zara smirked. "Too long, I guess."

Tommi didn't bother to answer. She held her breath as the guy's horse spooked at an advertising sign on the rail and almost ran past his distance. The rider hauled him back into line just in time, and they sailed over with inches to spare. Yeah, this guy could ride.

When the round was over, Tommi glanced at the scoreboard, where each rider's name and number were posted. "Scott Papadakis," she read aloud. "You were right."

"I'm always right." Zara was still smirking.

Tommi's gaze followed the guy down the alley leading out of the ring. The next rider was already heading to her first fence, but in the shadows of the alley Tommi spotted Jamie talking to Fitz.

"Looks like Fitz is on deck," Tommi said, forgetting all about the cute guy. "Do you see Kate anywhere? I know she wanted to see his round."

Zara glanced up toward the stands behind them. "Don't see her up there with the others. She's probably back at the stalls trying to do three things at once and lost track of the time. The girl is seriously type A."

"Yeah." Tommi pulled her phone out of her jacket pocket. "I'd better text her so she doesn't miss it."

Kate was helping Miguel, the head groom, scrub buckets when her cell phone buzzed. Blowing out an annoyed breath—why did the phone always go off when she was elbow deep in water?—she grabbed it and scanned the text that had just come in.

"Who's that?" Miguel asked.

"Tommi." Kate felt a flash of guilt, realizing she'd totally forgotten to go watch her friend's eq round. "She says Fitz is riding any minute now."

"Go." Miguel grabbed the bucket out of her hand and added it to his pile. "Hurry."

"But—" Kate began.

"Go!" Miguel urged.

Kate hesitated for another second, her gaze wavering between the buckets and Miguel's face. Then she smiled her thanks and took off at a jog, trying not to think about the million other things she should be doing right now. The show had only officially started yesterday, and Kate was already stressed. Mrs. Walsh's mare hadn't finished her breakfast that morning and was on colic watch, someone had forgotten to pack the extra clipper blades, and a dog tied up over by the next set of stalls was driving everyone crazy with its nonstop barking. Grooming at Indoors was turning out to be just like doing it at a regular show—times ten.

Kate burst into the arena and glanced around. Fitz was on his horse watching the rider in the ring, but when he spotted her he gave her a thumbs-up and smiled. She smiled back, relieved. She'd made it!

Hearing her name, she looked around and saw Tommi and Zara waving at her from a few rows up. She hurried to join them, sliding into the empty seat beside Zara just as Fitz rode into the ring.

"Woo-hoo, go Fitz, you magnificent bastard!" Zara cheered, pumping her fist.

Kate laughed nervously, leaning forward and keeping her gaze trained on Fitz as he picked up the canter. He looked calm and confident out there, not to mention handsome in his dark jacket and tall boots.

"Hastings looks sharp," Tommi commented. "Probably a good thing Fitz leased him for finals instead of making River do it again."

"Yeah," Kate agreed, holding her breath as the big bay horse cleared the first fence in his usual smooth form.

Fitz owned half a dozen horses, including an old warrior of an eq horse that had been jumping around at finals since Jamie was a junior. The previous year, River had helped Fitz come close to a ribbon in several of the finals. But over the past year, everyone had noticed that the old gelding was slowing down, the years and countless jumps finally catching up with him. Kate knew it couldn't have been an easy decision to retire him from the big eq in Fitz's second-to-last junior year, but that was what had happened. These days, River did a few easy lessons per week with the less experienced kids where the fences were lower, spending the rest of his time relaxing in turnout with Fitz's semiretired children's hunter. Kate knew that many riders would have sold both horses once they couldn't perform at the level required, or at least sent them away to a cheaper retirement home. But Fitz was loyal to his old friends, and didn't mind spending his money—well, his parents' money—to keep them in the style to which they were accustomed. That was just one of the things Kate loved about him.

Luckily, retiring his eq horse didn't mean Fitz couldn't be competitive. After all, the division was judged on the rider, not the horse. He'd qualified on a variety of mounts, including his multitalented junior jumper, the greenie intended as River's replacement, and a couple of Jamie's sale horses. When finals drew closer, he'd leased Hastings, an experienced eq horse owned by a friend of Jamie's. Kate hadn't asked how much the lease cost and didn't really want to know, although HorseShowSecrets had speculated that the total cost for all four finals was somewhere in the six figures.

Kate couldn't imagine spending that much for a handful of shows, but she had to admit that the horse was giving Fitz his money's worth so far. He cleared the next few fences just as easily as the first, making the tight turn after the combination with no problem at all. She held her breath as he approached the second-to-last obstacle, a weird-looking log vertical that she'd heard had been giving a lot of riders trouble.

"Whee!" Zara said as the horse cleared it. "He made that look easy."

As the pair sailed over the final fence, Tommi leaped to her feet and let out a loud whoop, pumping her fist. Zara stuck two fingers in her mouth and whistled. Kate stood and applauded, smiling with relief.

"Wow, that looked great," she said.

"You're telling me." Tommi glanced at her. "If he rides his

second round anything like that one, he'll end up top twenty for sure."

Zara grinned. "And we can all say we knew him when. Come on, let's go find Mr. Hot Stuff."

Kate followed the other two girls down the stairs. They reached the alley just as Fitz swung down from the saddle. He was grinning from ear to ear.

"That's what I'm talking about!" he cried when he saw them, rushing over, grabbing Kate, and swinging her around in a full circle before setting her back on her feet.

She laughed breathlessly. "Careful, you'll scare the horses!"

"Nice job, Hall." Tommi stepped forward and clapped Fitz on the back. "I didn't think you had it in you."

He grinned at her. "Yes you did, Aaronson," he teased. "You've always known I was a superior specimen of studly equitationship."

Kate felt her phone vibrate in her pocket. "Hang on, Javier's calling," she told Fitz and the others. "Hello?" she said into the phone.

"Kate? You busy?" The young groom sounded stressed. "Because the farrier just showed up to put that pony's shoe back on, and I'm supposed to be lunging one of the other ponies right now—"

"It's okay, I'm on my way. Be there in three." Kate hung up and slid her phone back into her pocket.

"Don't say it," Fitz pleaded playfully, grabbing her around the waist again. "I wanted to go celebrate my awesome first round—and distract myself from getting nervous for the next one."

"Sorry, I've got to go." Kate stood on tiptoes to plant a quick kiss on his lips. "Congrats again."

She pulled away and hurried off, trying not to listen to her friends laughing and having fun behind her.

FOUR

▬▬ ▬▬ ▬▬ ▬▬ ▬▬

A few days later, Tommi was back in the stands of the main arena. The equitation championships were long over—Fitz had finished in sixth place, which had thrilled everyone. Tommi hadn't placed or even gotten a callback, as she'd expected. But that was okay; she'd already mentally moved on to Harrisburg, at least as far as the eq was concerned. She and Orion would show them all how it was done then. In the meantime, she was focused on her upcoming hunter division.

At that very moment, however, she wasn't thinking about eq *or* hunters. One of the show's few jumper classes was under way in the ring, and Legs was supposed to be coming in for his round soon. Tommi couldn't wait to see him. She'd received a couple of e-mails from his new owner saying how thrilled she was with the horse, but Tommi hadn't actually laid eyes on Legs since the sale was finalized.

Even so, she recognized him the second he came into the ring—on his toes as usual. Tommi smiled; he looked good.

She felt like a proud parent as she watched Legs do his

thing on course. He threw in a small buck between the first and second jumps, but his rider stuck it easily, and after that Legs didn't put a hoof wrong. He cleared every jump, easy and fast, not even peeking at the liverpool or the spooky jump at the far end of the ring that had caused several refusals in the time Tommi had been watching.

As he finished and left the ring, Tommi's smile faded. She leaned on the rail, not really seeing the next horse enter. Legs would probably never be a children's packer, but it was obvious that her time with him had done him good. He was a lot more adjustable, a lot more confident. Seeing him in person made her all too aware of the time that had passed since she'd sold him—the time that was *still* passing. She only had one more year as a junior rider in front of her. Tommi had never been a huge fan of thinking too hard about the future. What was the point? Nobody really knew what was going to happen.

But now? The future was hurtling toward her, and nothing was going to stop it. If Tommi wanted to have any say in how her life was going to go for the next few years, she couldn't let her father drag his feet any longer. She needed to get her plans back on track, and start looking for the next project horse to make up and sell. Maybe if she found a promising one, she could make another presentation to her father like the one she'd done for Legs. Maybe that would convince him to move forward with their business venture. Maybe it would even convince him that she wasn't destined to follow his footsteps to Georgetown University and a career in the business world.

A burst of applause snapped Tommi out of her thoughts. Glancing into the ring, she saw that another horse had just finished its round.

Turning away from the rail, she started climbing the steps leading up to the top rows of the stands. That was where most of Pelham Lane's juniors had been camped out all day, studying while they had the chance.

Marissa, Zara, Fitz, and Summer had their books, notes, and other school stuff spread out all over the place. Marissa was bent over her laptop, though the other three seemed to be taking a break. Fitz was sucking down an energy drink, while the two girls were leaning back in their seats, watching the action in the ring.

"We saw Legs go," Zara said when Tommi arrived. "He did awesome!"

"Yeah." Tommi sat down next to her, pulling her schoolbag out from under the seat.

Zara sat up and peered at her. "What's wrong? You don't seem too happy about it."

Tommi unzipped her bag. "I am. It's just, seeing him reminded me I'm supposed to be looking for my next project."

"You're doing another one? Cool," Fitz said.

"That's the plan." Tommi lifted one shoulder. "So if you guys hear of any, like, promising young horses that might work for me, let me know, okay?"

"Will do," Fitz said, while Summer and Zara nodded.

Tommi didn't have much hope that any of the trio would be likely to turn up a viable prospect. Summer rarely paid attention to anything that didn't directly benefit herself, and the other two weren't exactly the most pragmatic of shoppers. Exhibit A? The way Fitz had snapped up that off-the-track Thoroughbred Kate had noticed at a little local show. It looked like that one could actually pay off, since the horse was really nice. But Tommi had the distinct feeling that if the beast Kate had commented on had been a donkey or a draft horse, Fitz might have bought that, too.

Still, you never could tell who could hear something interesting. Tommi glanced over at Marissa, who knew just about everybody on the circuit and liked to keep up with all the news at the shows. She might actually have a shot of hearing about something that would work for Tommi.

"Marissa?" Tommi said. "Did you hear what I said? I'm looking for a new project horse."

"What?" Marissa finally looked up from her computer. "Oh, okay. But listen, you'll never believe what just popped up on HorseShowSecrets. Check it out—it's about Joy!"

"Joy?" Fitz looked intrigued. "As in, our assistant trainer Joy?"

"That's the one." Marissa turned the laptop so they could all see the screen. "See? It talks about how everyone at Pelham Lane is saying Joy hasn't been herself lately. And how there could be lots of reasons for her weird behavior—like maybe she's spying for another barn, or just got diagnosed with something horrible, or is plotting to push Jamie out and take over Pelham Lane."

Tommi rolled her eyes. "Is that really what passes for horse show gossip these days? The blogger must be getting desperate. Joy hardly ever even goes to shows."

"I know, right? Who cares about her." Summer bent forward to grab a candy bar out of her bookbag. "Tommi's right, the blog is supposed to be about the shows, and duh, one of the biggest shows of the year is happening right now!" She waved her candy bar at the arena around them.

"Maybe that means the blogger isn't here at Cap Challenge," Fitz speculated. "Maybe he or she isn't even really an A circuit insider."

"Ooh," Tommi put in. "The plot thickens."

If the others noticed her sarcasm, they didn't show it. Marissa was shaking her head. "There was a post yesterday about that trainer from Alabama or Georgia or wherever who melted down when his fancy green hunter didn't pin, remember?" she said. "Only someone who was here could have known about that."

"Good point," Fitz agreed. "Still, it's kind of weird that something about Pelham Lane is coming out now."

"I know, right?" Marissa grabbed her phone. "Let's text Dani and see if she's at the barn today. Maybe she can stalk Joy and find out the truth."

Summer gasped. "Wait—what if *Joy* is the blogger? That would totally explain why there's a post about her! And Jamie could have mentioned that Georgia trainer when he called home."

"Are you for real?" Fitz shook his head. "I had to teach Joy how to set up the barn's online bank account last year. I seriously doubt she's mastered the art of blogging since then."

Summer looked wounded. "Whatever. It's just a theory, okay?"

"Chill, Summer." Marissa's thumbs were flying over her phone's tiny keyboard. "He's just giving you a hard time. We're all wondering who's behind that blog."

"Yeah, no kidding," Zara muttered.

Tommi glanced at her, realizing she'd been uncharacteristically quiet for the past few minutes. Was she still upset over that piece about her father? Zara noticed her glance, but turned away to grab a math textbook.

That reminded Tommi that she was behind on her own studies. "Tell Dani I said hi," she told Marissa.

She pulled her laptop and physics book out of her bag. The jumper class was still going on in the ring, and it was tempting to chill for a while and watch. But Tommi knew she couldn't let her grades slip even a little. If she did, her dad was likely to use that as an excuse to back out of their deal. And Tommi definitely didn't want to give him any excuses.

"Easy, buddy," Kate murmured as she checked the girth of the medium pony dancing in place beside her. "Nothing to be scared of here, Dazzle baby. You're a brave boy."

That was a lie, and Kate knew it. The pony, a dapple gray Welsh cross, was just as high-strung as he was fancy. He tended to snort and leap around and sometimes buck his eight-year-old owner off if someone didn't school him in the ring before his division started. That was Kate's job, and it was one she normally enjoyed. Dazzle was fun to ride despite his quirks, and if she did her thing now he was all but guaranteed to place in the pony hunters the next day.

Or later *that* day, technically. Kate stifled a yawn, trying not to think about what time it was. She'd waited until the wee hours of the morning to school the pony, hoping it would be easier to settle him in while the ring was relatively quiet.

There were a couple of other riders still schooling out there, but the atmosphere was nothing like it had been earlier in the evening, when the whole place was a sea of riders, lungers, and trainers yelling orders or advice.

Kate glanced up at the stands. They were also mostly empty at this hour, though Kate spotted two or three juniors bent over laptops or schoolbooks. Trying to squeeze in some studying whenever they could, she guessed.

The thought brought on a pang of guilt. Kate had been so busy that she'd barely cracked open a book all week. She would have to do something about that. She could only imagine what Mr. Barron would say if she turned up after the show with none of her chemistry homework done. Not to mention that five-page English paper she was supposed to write, or those problem sets for trig, or . . .

The pony jerked his head to one side, yanking the reins out of Kate's hands and Kate's mind back to the here and now. She couldn't afford to get spacey at the moment, sleep or no sleep.

"Okay, here we go—easy now . . ." Kate gathered up the reins, then stuck her left foot in the stirrup and swung carefully aboard. Dazzle scooted forward a few steps, but stopped when Kate asked.

Kate rubbed his withers, then picked up the reins and nudged him forward toward the gate. The pony felt quick and nervous under her, but that was normal for him. It was also normal for Kate to feel like a giant while riding him—he was definitely a *lot* shorter than Fable or Flame or most of the other horses she rode. That was why Joy usually schooled the mediums at home, since she was several inches shorter than Kate and almost as slim.

Kate waited for a beefy chestnut to pass at an easy canter, then sent the pony into a trot. The gait started off rough, but Dazzle soon settled into his usual long, sweeping stride.

For the next few minutes, Kate kept the pony trotting, throwing in changes of direction, circles, serpentines, some basic lateral work, and anything else she could think of to occupy his busy little mind. It was warm in the ring, and before long the pony had worked up a sweat. Kate started to calculate how long it would take her to bathe him after the workout, then walk him dry and get him groomed. She would need to have him ready to go by the time the braider arrived at—what time had she said she was coming again? Kate tried to focus on what Jamie had told her earlier, but forgot about that when Dazzle suddenly veered off the rail and tossed his head.

"Easy," Kate said, reeling him in and nudging him back over.

The pony soon settled and Kate stifled a yawn, deciding there was no point in trying to guess when she might actually make it to sleep that night. Still, she couldn't help wondering what time her friends had gone to bed. Zara had said something about trying to hit some party the juniors from a different barn were throwing, but Tommi and Marissa had seemed skeptical. In any case, Kate was sure that all of them had been snoring away in their hotel rooms for at least the past couple of hours. And would probably still be sound asleep when Kate arrived back at the showgrounds to help the grooms feed . . .

Realizing she was sinking into a pity party, she did her best to shake it off and focus on what she was doing. This was what she'd signed on for, right? This was the life she loved, living and breathing horses and showing and all the rest. The only way she could be a part of this world was through hard work and long hours. Sometimes *really* long hours.

And that was okay. Even at times like this, when she was so tired she was yawning every ten seconds and could hardly muster the strength to keep her grip on the reins, she felt lucky and grateful to be here. It wasn't easy, but it was her life—the only life she could imagine. If her parents and her teachers could just understand that and maybe cut her some slack once in a while . . .

"Heads up!" a voice rang out.

With a burst of adrenaline, Kate realized she'd drifted into the path of the lumbering chestnut as it headed toward a jump. She quickly kicked Dazzle into a canter to circle out of the way.

"Sorry!" she called to the other rider.

Shaking her head to clear it, she did her best to banish all thoughts of schoolwork, her parents, and the rest. She could worry about that stuff later. Right now she had a job to do.

FIVE

"I can't believe it's Saturday already—it feels like we just got here like two seconds ago, I swear," Marissa chattered, her words coming so fast Zara had trouble following them. "Where did the week go?"

"You got me." Zara grabbed the rag out of Marissa's hand before she could spook her cross-tied horse by flapping it around. The girl got nervous before every class, but this was ridiculous. "Trust me, I'm not exactly thrilled about going back to school in two days. I doubt I've even finished half the crap my teachers gave me to do."

"You and me both," Tommi put in, glancing up from the next set of cross-ties, where she was tightening her junior hunter's girth.

Summer was leaning against the wall nearby, watching Tommi and Marissa get ready for their large junior hunter under saddle class, though Zara noticed she didn't seem to feel any need to help like Zara and Fitz were doing.

"I got all my homework done yesterday," Summer announced,

studying her manicure. "I wanted to enjoy the last weekend of the show without school stuff getting in my way."

"Well, aren't you special," Zara said with a snort. "I guess every barn needs a resident nerd."

Summer frowned, while everyone else laughed. Well, *almost* everyone. Kate was dashing around helping with this and that—rubbing a little more oil on the horses' hooves, wiping an invisible spot off Marissa's saddle flap, whatever. It made Zara tired to watch her, especially since Kate seemed even more stressed than the two people who were actually about to ride in the class.

"We'd better hurry." Tommi pushed back the cuff of her jacket to check her watch. "Where'd I put my bridle?"

"Here it is." Kate lunged across the grooming area and grabbed a bridle off a hook. "I'll help you."

"Can you help me, too?" Marissa begged, clutching her own bridle so hard her knuckles were white. "I'm a total fumble fingers when I'm nervous."

"Got you covered," Zara said, stepping forward. She took the bridle from Marissa and slung the reins over her horse's head. "Unclip him on that side and get the halter off—I'll do the rest."

Marissa's smile was insanely grateful. "Thanks, Zara."

"Where are all the grooms, anyway?" Summer sounded vaguely annoyed. "Shouldn't they be here helping you? Isn't that what they get paid for?"

"Hello! Kate's standing right in front of you." Fitz pointed at Kate, who was helping Tommi wrestle with her hunter. Toccata was clearly picking up on the nervous energy zipping around him and had started dancing in place.

"Okay, but she's not really a groom." Summer shot Kate a dismissive look. "Just a working student."

At that moment a girl around their age came rushing down the aisle, trying to shrug on her jacket as she went. Zara had seen her around all week, which meant she probably rode with one of the other barns stabled nearby.

"Are you guys in the hack?" the girl blurted out breathlessly. "Because we're supposed to be out there right now. They said if we—hey, aren't you Zara Trask? You know, Zac's daughter?" She stopped dead in front of Zara, the panic on her face suddenly replaced by naked curiosity. Her gaze slid toward the other girls, quickly looking each of them up and down.

"Zara Trask? Nope, never heard of her," Zara said, deadpan.

A muffled announcement came over the loudspeaker—something about a five-minute warning. The girl let out a squeak of terror. With one last curious glance at Zara and the others, she raced off.

"Looks like everyone's still wondering which of you ladies is Zac's jailbait, huh?" Fitz's tone was light, but Zara was pretty sure she actually saw a hint of sympathy in his eyes. "Some people really need to get a life."

"You're telling me," Zara muttered.

Summer finally glanced up from her own fingernails. "You can't blame people for being curious about something like that," she said. "I mean, for a second I even wondered when I first read that post." When Zara glared at her, she opened her pale blue eyes wide. "What? It's not like it couldn't be true."

"It's not," Zara told her through gritted teeth. "Trust me."

"Oh, I totally believe you," Summer assured her, suddenly sounding more like her usual suck-up self. "I'm just saying, I can sort of understand why other people might believe something like that."

"Whatever." Zara tightened the bridle's noseband a little too abruptly, causing Marissa's placid hunter to lift his head in surprise. Giving the horse a pat by way of apology, Zara glanced around at the others. "Anyway, I'm definitely over it."

"How do you think Joy feels?" Fitz grinned. "Everyone thinks she's either scamming her boss or has, like, an inoperable brain tumor."

"I know, right?" Marissa fastened her helmet strap. "It's a good thing Joy never gets on the Internet unless she absolutely has to. She probably doesn't even know about all the rumors."

"Whatever," Zara said again. "I just wish *I* didn't know about that blog. I'm sick of everyone at the stupid show asking me about it."

Marissa looked sympathetic. "Don't worry. All you have to do is wait for the next superjuicy rumor to come along, and everyone will forget about your dad."

"What if I don't want to wait that long?" Zara was feeling more irritable by the second. "Maybe I should do something about it *now*."

"Like what?" Fitz raised an eyebrow. "Track down the blogger and pull his hair out? Or her hair—you know, whichever." He shrugged. "Anyway, good luck with that. I mean, if nobody's figured out who's writing that blog by now, I'm not sure we're ever going to know."

That gave Zara an idea. So far, the blogger pretty much had the entire A circuit at his or her mercy. That needed to change, and if nobody else was going to make it happen, it seemed to be up to Zara. "Don't count on it," she told Fitz. "Because that's *exactly* what I'm going to do."

"Pull the blogger's hair out?" Summer sounded alarmed.

"Maybe." Zara shot her a wicked grin. "But first, I'm going to figure out who's behind that freaking blog and out them to the world!"

Tommi wasn't paying much attention to the conversation going on around her. She was focused on the coming class. Her hunter, Toccata, was a rock star over jumps, and he definitely had the movement to do well in the hack, too. But sometimes it was a challenge to keep him focused in a ring full of other horses. Tommi only hoped she was up to that challenge this time. They'd done well enough over fences that she was fairly confident that there would be a champion or reserve champion in it for them if they placed anywhere in the top six in the under saddle.

"We'd better get a move on," she said, pulling on her gloves. "I want to make sure Toccata gets to take a look around before the class starts."

"I'm ready." Marissa let out a nervous giggle. "Here goes nothing!"

"Don't worry, Miles will take care of you." Fitz gave Marissa's horse a fond slap on the neck. "Now get out there and kick some butt, you two!"

Soon Tommi and Marissa were mounted and walking their horses toward the gate of the outdoor ring where the class was being held. The day was overcast but warm, and the horses seemed happy to be outside. "Hold up," Kate said, hurrying over to wipe Tommi's boots.

"Thanks." Tommi flashed her a smile, grateful as always for her friend's attention to detail. Then she reached forward and gave Toccata a stroke on the neck. "Let's go get 'em, baby."

She rode into the ring, automatically guiding Toccata to an open spot on the rail while scanning the competition. Most of the riders' faces were familiar from seeing them in the division all year, though there were also quite a few from other parts of the country who only came east for the big shows. Tommi's gaze caught on one particular member of the latter group. It was Scott, the guy she'd noticed in the eq last weekend.

Interesting. She hadn't seen all of yesterday's jumping trips and hadn't realized he was in this division. Her gaze lingered on him as he sent his horse, a big, elegant chestnut with a crooked blaze and four high whites, into a gorgeous daisy-cutting trot. Nice.

Then Tommi heard hoofbeats coming up fast behind her. She glanced back just in time to steer Toccata to the inside and avoid a fast-moving gray with a wild look in its eyes and a nervous girl in the tack.

"Sorry!" the rider on the gray called in a shaky voice as she thundered past.

Tommi took a deep breath and half-halted, making sure Toccata was still with her. That had been close, and Tommi knew she'd better not let herself get distracted again. Toccata was way too easily rattled for her to lose focus just because a cute guy went trotting past.

The PA system clicked on, causing Toccata to spurt forward. "Walk, please, all walk," the announcer said.

"Here we go," Tommi whispered, glancing around to make sure she was in a clear spot where the judge could see Toccata's beautiful gait.

From that point on, her famous focus took over—mostly. Once or twice, Tommi couldn't resist seeking out Scott Papadakis to see how he was doing. His horse was just as fancy as she'd thought, and Scott was skilled enough to show off his mount to his very best advantage. If the pair had done anywhere near as well over fences, Tommi knew they'd give her and Toccata some competition for those championship ribbons.

At the end of the class, Tommi found herself next to Scott in the lineup. He gave his horse a pat, then smiled over at her. "You're Tommi Aaronson, right?" he said. "You were looking good out there."

"Thanks. You too." Tommi returned his smile. "Nice horse."

Before Scott could respond, the announcer started reading off the placings. Marissa finished out of the ribbons, but Tommi pinned third and Scott first.

In the end, Scott was champion, while Tommi had to settle for reserve.

"Congrats," she told him when they had finished the award presentation. "Guess you must have laid down some impressive trips yesterday. Sorry I missed them."

"Me too." He grinned at her. "I caught yours, though. I like to keep up with the competition."

"And?" Tommi cocked her head and raised an eyebrow.

He smiled, his dark eyes twinkling with a hint of mischief. "Not bad. Not as good as me, but not bad."

"Oh yeah?" Tommi grinned. Competitive, *and* with a sense of humor? Yes, please. "We'll have to see if you can back that up at Harrisburg." She smirked. "*If* you managed to qualify, that is."

"Oh, we'll be there." Scott leaned forward and patted his horse, still grinning. "And we're definitely up for a rematch."

By then Jamie was heading toward Tommi, along with Miguel, who was holding Toccata's cooler.

"Nice," Jamie said, grabbing Toccata's bridle as the sensitive horse starting jigging in reaction to the crowd outside the ring. "You kept him settled and showed him at his best. No complaints from me. This judge always uses the best trot, and I guess she thought the red horse's trot was a little better."

"Yeah. It's cool, win some lose some." Tommi gave Toccata a pat, then unhooked her helmet. She hated losing and was the first to beat herself up when she screwed up a class, but she really did feel good about this one. She'd been showing long enough to know that Jamie was right—sometimes the judge just liked another horse better, even when yours was at his best. That was showing.

As Jamie turned away to talk to Marissa, Tommi's gaze slid toward Scott. He'd dismounted nearby and was discussing his performance with his trainer, a wiry older woman Tommi vaguely recognized.

Tommi dismounted and ran up her stirrups. "I'll take him for you." Miguel stepped forward to grab the horse's reins and hand Tommi her cell phone, which he'd held during the class.

"Thanks, Miguel." Tommi gave Toccata a scratch on the crest. Now that their division was over, it didn't matter if she messed up his braids—Miguel would be taking them out in a few minutes—so she dug her fingers in the way the horse liked. He lifted his head, his lower lip flapping with pleasure.

Then, as Miguel led Toccata away through the crowded gate area, Tommi looked around for her friends. Marissa was still talking to Jamie nearby, but Tommi didn't see the others. She did spot someone else, though. Scott was wandering toward her, his Samshield still perched on his head with the strap undone and his jacket unbuttoned. His show gloves were peeking out of the pocket of his breeches.

"Hey," he greeted her. "So I'm Scott, by the way."

Tommi didn't bother to tell him she already knew that. "Nice to meet you, Scott. So how come I haven't seen you at the shows before?" she asked, leaning against the ring fence.

"First time here. I'm an Indoors virgin." Scott grinned. "See, my dad has all these crazy rules of life that he forces me to live by. One of them is that anything worth doing is worth working for, which he somehow interpreted as meaning I couldn't come east for the big shows until I had straight As for at least a year."

"So I take it you hit the books?"

"Absolutely." Scott pulled off his helmet and tucked it under his arm, shooting Tommi a sidelong look as he ran a hand through his dark hair. "I *always* get what I want in the end. Crazy dad or not."

"That's funny—so do I." Tommi's mind flashed to her business plans. "Your dad sounds a lot like my dad, actually."

Scott shrugged. "They probably know each other. Mine's CEO of MacroNet. He's always dealing with Wall Street guys like your dad."

Okay, now Tommi knew why Scott's last name had seemed vaguely familiar. MacroNet was one of the most successful companies in Silicon Valley, which meant Scott's father probably had almost as much money as Tommi's did.

That didn't impress her much. And her family name didn't seem to impress Scott much, either, which Tommi actually found kind of a turn-on. So many guys got all weird as soon as they realized Tommi was one of *those* Aaronsons, part of the family that owned half of New York. It got old.

"Do you have your phone on you?" Scott asked.

Tommi reached into her pocket and pulled out her cell. She'd switched it off during the class, but now she turned it back on.

Then she held it up. "Why?"

Scott plucked it out of her hand. "I'm sending myself a text," he said as his thumbs tapped out a message. "That way you'll have my number, and I'll have yours."

"Very efficient." Tommi held back a smile. Okay, yes, this guy was seriously intriguing. That didn't mean she had to let him know it. "So what are you expecting us to do with each other's numbers?"

Scott handed her the phone, his hand brushing hers and lingering for a moment. "Well, I was thinking . . . ," he began.

"Tommi!" Fitz burst out of the crowd and made a beeline toward her. "Hey, there you are. I was afraid you'd already left."

Scott quickly pulled his hand away and stepped back. Tommi turned to face Fitz, who seemed totally clueless that he might have interrupted something. "What is it?" she asked, trying not to sound impatient or flustered.

"I've got some news," Fitz said. "I was just talking to this girl I know from Kara Parodi's barn."

"Don't you know *all* the girls from Kara Parodi's barn?" Tommi cut in. "And every other barn, too?"

Fitz put a hand over his heart. "You wound me, Aaronson. You know I'm not like that anymore."

"If you say so." Tommi glanced at Scott. Or the spot where Scott had been standing, anyway. Tommi frowned slightly as she realized he'd slipped away. Oh well. "What's the big news?" she asked Fitz.

"Anna says Kara has a horse for sale," Fitz said. "Green, but with tons of potential. She's got a full barn already, so she's willing to let it go for an awesome price. Thought you might want to check it out."

"Thanks for the tip." Tommi smiled at him. "I'll definitely check it out."

She felt a shiver run through her. Could this be fate, or some kind of sign? Tommi didn't usually believe in that stuff, but she had to wonder. Legs's new owner kept him at Kara Parodi's supersuccessful northern New Jersey show barn. What if Tommi's next prospect came from that very same barn?

Her phone buzzed in her hand, pulling her back to reality. Tommi glanced at the screen.

"That's not Kate, is it?" Fitz asked. "I'm supposed to be meeting her in the tack stall right now."

"No, it's not Kate." Tommi kept her voice calm, not wanting to invite any questions or teasing from Fitz.

But as soon as Fitz loped off, a smile spread across Tommi's face. Scott wanted to hang out that evening after the show. So this guy didn't waste time; another turn-on. Tommi only hesitated for a second before texting him back, suggesting they meet up in the lobby of her hotel.

Why not? She'd been single for a while—too long, really, now that she thought about it—and Scott seemed pretty cool. Definitely a lot more intriguing than the same old boring guys she'd gone to school with forever, anyway.

Not that she was looking for anything serious here. After all, she and Scott lived on opposite coasts. But still—what was the harm in a fun little fling?

SIX

Kate stared at her history textbook. The words swam before her eyes, seeming to rearrange themselves into nonsense syllables. She squeezed her eyes shut for a second and then opened them, glancing down at the indoor ring, where a large pony hunter was loping around the course.

"Ugh!" Zara muttered beside her. "Who ever decided to torture people by forcing them to learn algebra, anyway?"

She slammed her book shut with a bang. Kate glanced over. The two of them were the only Pelham Lane juniors hanging out in their usual study spot in the top few rows of the stands. Fitz had gone to find some food, Summer and Marissa had gotten bored and gone off to shop at the vendors' booths, and Kate wasn't sure where Tommi was. It felt a little strange to be alone with Zara. She was definitely part of the gang now, but she and Kate didn't hang out together much unless Tommi was there too, or Fitz, or some of the others.

Zara heaved a sigh and shoved her books away, leaning back against the row behind her and stretching her legs out onto the seats below. "Pony hunters," she said, glancing at the ring. "Okay, that might be the only thing even more boring than algebra."

Kate smiled uncertainly. Sometimes she still couldn't tell when Zara was joking. "Is algebra all you have left?" she asked, her gaze drifting back to her own textbook.

"Nah." Zara flicked a speck of hay off her jeans. "I've got a bunch of Spanish vocab to memorize, and some history essay questions, I think. Oh yeah, and I haven't even cracked open *The Scarlet Letter* yet, and I'm supposed to have the whole thing read by Monday." She made a face. "It's like our teachers don't want us to have any fun while we're away, so they pile on as much work as they possibly can."

"I know what you mean." Kate bit her lip, her mind skittering over her own list of unfinished homework. "So what are you going to do if you don't get everything done in time?"

"What am I going to do?" Zara laughed, seeming surprised by the question. "I don't know. Get yelled at by my teachers, I guess? Why do you think I'm doing algebra first? Ms. Rivera can *really* yell."

She didn't sound too worried. Kate wished she knew what that felt like. It was hard to be carefree when she knew the rest of her Indoor season might depend on keeping her teachers happy. Which reminded her, she shouldn't be sitting around chatting. Soon it would be time to start mixing the evening feed, and then she was supposed to school a couple of children's hunters to get them ready to show tomorrow, and after that there were about a million other things to do. Kate couldn't imagine when she'd find time to get back to her homework.

And she still had too much to hope to finish it all on the drive back up to New York. *Way* too much.

Her eyes had barely settled back on the page when her phone buzzed. "Is that you or me?" Zara asked, scrabbling for her bag.

"Me, I think. I hope it's not Miguel." Kate pulled out her phone. She sighed with relief when she saw that the text wasn't from the head groom. "It's Tommi."

"Tommi? Where is that girl, anyway?" Zara sat up and looked at Kate's phone. "She disappeared right after her hack class earlier, and I haven't seen her since."

Kate scanned the text. "She's trying out a horse in the outdoor schooling ring in, like, five minutes. She wants me to come watch and give her my opinion." She looked up at Zara. "I bet it's that greenie from Kara Parodi's barn. Fitz heard about it and thought it might work for Tommi's next project."

"What are we waiting for?" Zara hopped to her feet, grabbed her bag, and slung it over her shoulder. "Let's go check it out."

"But . . ." Kate hesitated, glancing at her history textbook. And the chemistry notes bulging out of her backpack. And the stack of other books and papers, most of which she'd barely touched.

Zara was already halfway down the stands. Shoving her backpack out of the way under the bench, Kate followed. She wasn't getting much done here anyway. Maybe a break would help clear her mind.

The day had gone gloomier since the last time Kate was outside, with massive gray clouds on the horizon signaling rain. But it was dry at the moment, and several people were riding in the outdoor schooling ring. Among them was a woman on a nice-looking liver chestnut with three white legs and a star. Tommi was standing at the rail watching the pair as they walked on a loose rein.

She glanced over as Kate and Zara joined her. "Oh good, you got my text," she said, sounding distracted. "Kara just got on."

Kate nodded, her eyes on the horse. "How old is it? Looks young."

"Five," Tommi replied. "Mare. Just imported from Holland."

"Nice," Zara said, leaning her elbows on the rail. "Love all the chrome. That's the only thing I'd change about Keeper if I could—he hardly has any white on him. Boring."

Kate watched as the trainer, a brisk woman in her late forties, sent the mare into a trot. The horse looked pretty good, but Kate knew looks could be deceiving—especially with a pro like Kara Parodi in the irons.

"Good trot," Kate said. "Hard to say how ridable she is till you try her, though."

Tommi nodded, not taking her eyes off the horse. For the next few minutes Kara put the mare through her paces, ending by popping her over a couple of small jumps. Finally the trainer pulled up in front of the girls.

"She's not doing courses yet," Kara said, giving the mare a pat. "She was actually bred for dressage, so they only put the basics on her over in Europe when it comes to jumping. But she's got talent—someone just needs to work with her a little. Want to take her for a spin?"

"Sure." Tommi grabbed her helmet, which was sitting on

the bench behind her. Then she ducked into the ring as Kara dismounted.

Kate and Zara watched without talking much as Tommi rode. Kara stayed in the ring, giving Tommi tips on how to bring out the best in the horse. Once again the mare looked pretty good for a greenie, though not quite as steady as she'd seemed with Kara, and Kate noticed Tommi frowning a couple of times. By the time she pulled up, Tommi looked uncertain.

"What do you think?" Kara asked.

"I'm not sure." Tommi gave the mare a pat, then glanced at Kate. "Do you mind if I have my friend Kate get on for a sec? She's one of the best riders at Jamie's barn, and I'd love a second opinion."

Kara raised an eyebrow as she followed Tommi's gaze. Kate felt her face go hot, all too aware of her ratty jeans stained with who-knew-what, her lopsided ponytail with hay stuck in it . . .

"No problem," Kara said.

Tommi smiled hopefully at Kate. "Do you mind?"

"Sure, that's fine." Kate ducked through the fence and walked over to the horse. The mare turned her head to nudge at her curiously, and Kate rubbed the horse's soft nose.

Tommi swung down from the saddle, then took off her helmet and handed it to Kate. "I think we're the same size, right?" she said.

"Close enough, I'm sure." Kate took the helmet rather gingerly. It was the latest model of GPA, which meant it had cost at least five times as much as Kate's own much more modest brain bucket.

Trying not to think about that, she strapped the helmet on, then accepted a leg up from Tommi while Kara held the horse's bridle. As soon as she was in the saddle, Kate forgot everything else, focusing on the horse beneath her.

"Good girl," she murmured as she quickly adjusted her stirrups.

"She likes a light hand," Kara told her. "Not too much leg either, unless she sees something that confuses her. Then you'll need to push her."

"Okay." Kate picked up the reins and gave the mare a nudge with her legs, sending her into a walk.

Within seconds, Kate knew that the trainer's comments had been an understatement. The mare was much greener and more difficult to ride than either the trainer or Tommi had made her look. She was also hyperaware of everything around her, from the horse doing trot circles at the other end of the schooling ring to the children's pony class going on in the main ring across the way to a bird on the fence nearby. Kate had to work to keep the mare's attention, and while her gaits were free and flowing and she did everything Kate asked, she never really felt relaxed through her body.

"Thanks," Kate said at last, halting beside Kara. "She's nice."

Kara nodded, taking the bridle as Kate dismounted. "Go ahead and talk to Tommi if you want," the trainer said. "I'll cool her out."

"Well?" Tommi asked when Kate walked over.

"She's—interesting." Kate took off Tommi's helmet and handed it back to her. "I mean, she has the movement for hunters, but I'm not sure whether her temperament's going to be a match. She seems awfully tense—maybe because she's young and inexperienced, or maybe just because that's who she is. Either way, she's definitely a lot trickier to ride than she looks."

"That's what I thought." Tommi grimaced. "I was kind of hoping it was just me."

Zara was listening with interest. "So what are you going to do? She's awfully fancy."

"I know." Tommi hesitated, watching the mare walk past with Kara. "The price is good, too. But I need to convince my dad I can make money on the next horse I buy, and I'm not sure this is the horse to do that with."

"Yeah." Kate tried not to resent the way Tommi talked so casually about buying and selling a horse like the one in front of them. The price in question might be "good" by Kara Parodi's standards, or Tommi's, or Zara's. That still put her as far out of reach as a brand-new Mercedes for someone like Kate.

"Too bad," Zara said. "Looks like she'd be a fun project for someone."

Just then Kara came over, the mare trailing along behind her. "Well?" the trainer said.

Tommi smiled. "Thanks for letting me try her, but I'm going to have to pass," she said. "She's a bit trickier than I'm looking for right now."

The trainer nodded, not seeming surprised by Tommi's response. "Yeah, I'm afraid she's going to be a tough sell," she said with a sigh. "Probably not the thing for a young rider like you."

"Right. Thanks again, though," Tommi said.

"Uh-huh." Kara Parodi wasn't looking at her anymore. Her keen hazel eyes had turned to study Kate. "I just figured out who you are," she said. "You're the girl who's been riding that big gray in the eq classes lately."

"Um, yeah," Kate stammered, unnerved by the way the trainer was looking at her.

"Oh, sorry, I should've introduced you," Tommi put in. "This is Kate Nilsen, Jamie's working student. She and Fable have been doing awesome in the eq."

Kara nodded. "You can really ride," she told Kate. "Are you going to be at Harrisburg?"

"Y-yes?" Kate's mind flashed briefly to her unfinished schoolwork, but she pushed that aside.

"Great. Any chance you'll be available to catch-ride?" Kara asked. "I've got a student with one too many horses qualified for the Large Juniors, and we're looking for a rider."

Kate was stunned. Was she hearing things, or had Kara Parodi just asked her to catch-ride one of her rich clients' fancy junior hunters? It didn't make sense. The woman ran a big, busy program. Didn't she have plenty of juniors in her own barn who'd be willing to step in?

"Kate would be perfect for that!" Tommi spoke up. "She can ride anything."

"Yeah." Zara grinned. "Jamie makes her ride the ones that send the rest of us screaming."

"Terrific." Kara looked pleased. "I should warn you—the horse in question is a sensitive ride. He's mostly fine outside, but he can be spooky in new places, especially indoors. And this will be his first time at Harrisburg." She shook her head. "None of my juniors want to deal with him, so we're looking for a confident rider who can give him a good experience."

"No problem," Tommi said. "Kate's great at giving confidence to anxious horses. If anyone can handle him, she can."

"I figured she could after watching her with this girl." Kara patted the mare, then turned to Kate. "What do you say?"

Kate had no idea how to respond. It would be amazing to get the chance to jump a good horse around in a real division at a big show—especially after a week spent stuck riding only in the schooling ring. And she actually enjoyed a horse that presented a bit of a challenge, so Kara's description didn't worry her at all. But wouldn't it be disloyal to Jamie to ride for another trainer?

"Um, I don't know," she stammered. "I'm not sure that—"

"She'll think about it," Tommi cut her off. "She has to check in with Jamie, see if the schedule works out."

"I understand." Kara checked her watch. "Let me know, all right? The horse will be coming to the show regardless—if you can't do it, one of my girls will just have to suck it up." With a quick laugh and a last nod to all three of them, she hurried off with the chestnut mare in tow.

Tommi spun to face Kate. "This is amazing!" she exclaimed. "Now I'm really glad I texted you."

Kate glanced around to make sure Kara Parodi was out of earshot. "But Kara's, like, one of Jamie's biggest rivals. Wouldn't it be weird for me to ride for her?"

Tommi waved a hand. "It's no big deal. Happens all the time."

"Yeah," Zara agreed. "There was this girl at my old barn who used to catch-ride for everyone, and our trainer was fine with it."

Tommi nodded. "I bet I even know the horse Kara's talking

about," she said. "It's probably that big bay Trakehner-type thing with the Arabian-looking head. I rode against him at Hounds Hollow in the Older Larges. He's super fancy, but the girl who owns him tries to slow everything down to a crawl, and he wouldn't go for that. Almost bucked her off in the under saddle."

"I think I remember that horse." Zara's eyes lit up. "He looked like fun! Kate, you should totally go for it."

Kate bit her lip. Were her friends right? She just wasn't sure. Jamie had done so much for her—he was the whole reason she was anywhere near an A circuit show right now. So what if he hadn't asked her to ride anything fancy at Indoors her first time out? Was that reason enough to go behind his back and accept a ride from someone else?

The buzz of her cell phone interrupted her thoughts. It was a text from Javier.

"Uh-oh," Kate said, scanning it. "Sounds like things are getting busy over at the stalls. I've got to go."

"Have fun," Tommi said.

"Want me to grab your books?" Zara offered. "I've got to go get mine anyway."

Kate gulped, remembering the schoolbooks she'd abandoned in the stands. And all the untouched homework contained within them. When was she ever going to finish it all?

"Thanks, that would be great," she told Zara. Trying to push her worries about school out of her mind, she hurried toward the stabling area.

"So if I make it to New York one of these days, will you give me a private guided tour?" Scott leaned across the table, the glow from the restaurant's kitschy glass-shaded overhead light bringing out reddish highlights in his dark hair.

"Maybe if you ask nicely." Tommi stirred another sugar into her iced tea, then took a sip. It was almost eleven, and she knew she needed to get to bed soon if she didn't want to be dead on her feet the next day. Not that it mattered that much—her divisions were over, and she didn't have to do anything more strenuous than pack up her hotel room and then spend the day cheering on the children's hunters from her barn.

Since neither Tommi nor Scott had a car at the show, they'd been stuck hanging out at the restaurant in Tommi's hotel. After a dinner of mediocre pasta, they'd lingered at the table so long their waiter had started giving them dirty looks. Scott had taken care of that by slipping the man some cash, and from then on the waiter seemed happy enough to keep bringing them as many more drinks and nachos as they wanted.

Scott licked his finger and used it to snag the last few nacho crumbs off the plate sitting between them. "If you ever come west, I'll show you around out there," he said. "You can even come to my barn and hop on my horse to find out what a real hunter feels like." He grinned.

"Oh, I know what one feels like," Tommi countered with a smirk. "I just hope someday you get someone to take pity on you and put you on a real eq horse. I mean, my horse tripped— can happen to anyone. What's your excuse for not pinning?"

"Ouch." Scott collapsed back into his chair as if he'd just been shot. "I can't believe you'd go there after I poured my heart out about that."

Tommi just smiled and took another sip of her drink. True,

Scott had spent a while complaining that his eq horse hadn't turned out to be nearly as experienced as its seller had assured him it was. Somehow, though, Tommi didn't think teasing Scott about it was going to wound him all that much. In fact, she'd be surprised if he didn't turn up on a reliable world-beater next year. Like her, he had one more season as a junior, and she suspected he'd make the most of it—just like she was planning to do.

Then again, maybe a professional eq horse would be too boring for him. That was another thing the two of them seemed to have in common. Like Tommi, Scott wasn't afraid of a challenge.

Just then the waiter approached. "What else can I get for you two?" he asked, whisking the empty nacho plate out from in front of them.

"More nachos?" Scott asked Tommi. "Or some dessert, maybe?"

Tommi shook her head. "I'd better call it a night. I'm supposed to be back at the show early tomorrow, and if I show up looking like a zombie I'll scare the horses."

Scott grinned, but he looked disappointed. "You sure?"

"Yeah." Tommi stood up. "It's been fun, though. Or at least as much fun as you can have in suburban Maryland. Maybe we can do it again in Harrisburg."

"Sounds like a plan." Scott pulled out his wallet, selected a credit card, and handed it to the waiter. "I'll be back to sign for that in a sec," he told the man. "Gotta walk the lady to the elevator." He hesitated, raising an eyebrow at Tommi. "Unless you want to wait for me to settle up, and I can walk you to your room?"

"Elevator's fine," Tommi said.

Scott shrugged. "Can't blame a guy for trying, right?" he told the waiter with a wink. "Be right back."

They headed out of the restaurant, which was empty except for a couple of businessmen sitting at the bar. "Thanks for coming," the bored-looking hostess said in a bored-sounding voice as they passed her station.

"Thanks," Tommi said.

Scott opened the door for her. The lobby was just as deserted as the restaurant. A single employee was bent over a computer behind the desk and barely looked up as they passed.

When they reached the elevators, Tommi stopped and turned to face Scott. "So . . . ," she said as she hit the button to summon an elevator. "Give me a call when you hit Harrisburg."

"Don't worry, I will." Scott took a step closer. "Good night, Tommi."

Tommi leaned forward as he bent to kiss her. His lips touched hers softly at first, then pressed more insistently, making her heart thump. The *ding*-and-*whoosh* of the elevator arriving interrupted the moment, making them both pull away.

"Good night," Tommi said, feeling a little breathless as she stepped into the elevator. Scott smiled and raised one hand, his eyes locked on hers until the doors slid shut to separate them.

SEVEN

"Rise and shine, my love!"

Zara groaned, trying to convince herself that her mother's overly peppy voice was part of the dream she'd been having—something about her algebra teacher chasing her up the New Jersey Turnpike on a fire-breathing horse . . .

Then she felt a sharp poke on her shoulder. "Ow!" she blurted out, her eyes flying open.

Her mother's face was peering down at her, already powdered and plucked and ready to face a movie star's day of getting ogled and photographed everywhere she went. "Time to get up," Gina said. "Mickey's waiting to drive you to school."

"School?" Zara shoved herself into a semiupright position and rubbed her eyes. "Actually, I was thinking I might skip it today."

"Think again," her mother said briskly, yanking back the covers. "We already told you—if you're expecting to attend all these horse shows during the school year, you'll have to prove you can keep up with your work."

Zara waited until her mother turned away, then rolled her eyes. Since when had Gina Girard, famous for playing all sorts of characters from carefree party girls to gorgeous but dedicated career women, decided to audition for the one role nobody would ever believe her in—superresponsible soccer mom?

"Fine," Zara muttered, climbing out of bed and fumbling for her slippers. "I'm going."

When she got downstairs, showered and dressed for school, someone had set out bagels with all the fixings on the sleek modern dining table. Mickey, her favorite member of her father's entourage, was lounging in one of the chairs, a half-full cup of coffee in one hand and an unlit cigarette in the other. He never seemed to eat much, which was probably how he pulled off that gaunt seventies-era punk-throwback look he had going.

"Morning, Z-Girl," he said in his raspy voice. "Better eat fast if you want to be on time."

"Oh, she does," Gina called out from across the room, where she was scribbling a note on the whiteboard near the phone. "She *definitely* wants to be on time."

"It's okay. I'm not that hungry." Zara grabbed an empty mug and poured herself a cup of coffee from the De'Longhi on the sideboard. She glanced around the main room, surprised to see that she, Mickey, and Gina were the only ones there. It was unusual to see the place without at least three or four of her father's lackeys hanging out doing whatever they did. Which, as far as Zara could tell, was pretty much nothing. "Where is everyone?" she asked, dumping a couple of sugars into her mug. "Where's Zac?"

"Still asleep." Mickey took a sip of his coffee. "He was up late last night."

"That makes two of us." Zara shot her mother an annoyed look. It had taken forever to get things packed up at the show the day before. On top of that, they'd run into a serious delay on the turnpike on the way home—some kind of tractor-trailer jackknife or something that had backed up traffic for miles. They hadn't arrived back at Pelham Lane until almost midnight, and Tommi had insisted on helping unload the horses before driving herself, Fitz, Summer, and Zara back into Manhattan.

Not that Gina cared about any of that. If Zara started complaining, it would just set her mother off on one of her boring stories about various all-nighters and other feats of human endurance she'd experienced on movie sets through the years. Even first-period history class had to be better than that.

Zara drained her coffee in about three gulps, ignoring the burn in her throat. "Okay, let's go," she told Mickey. "I'm ready."

She actually woke up a little during the drive to school. Mickey was good for that. For one thing, he drove like a maniac, cutting off other vehicles left and right and endangering pedestrians at every turn. That would get the adrenaline pumping if anything could. Besides that, his stories were actually interesting, unlike her mother's—mostly because he left in all the gory details.

By the time she walked into Drummond's echoing, stone-floored lobby, Zara was feeling almost awake. She stopped at her locker to dump most of her books, then went to look for Tommi.

She found her at her own locker. "You made it," Tommi said with a yawn. She bent closer to the little mirror stuck inside the locker door, slicking on some lip gloss. "I thought you might come in late."

"Not a chance, with both my parents home for a change."

Zara leaned against the next locker. "I don't know why they're so gung-ho about school, anyway. Zac barely made it through high school, and my mom doesn't exactly use her college degree in art history on a daily basis."

"I know what you mean." Tommi capped her lip gloss and stuck it on her locker shelf. When she turned around, Zara noticed she had a weird look on her face.

"What?" Zara peered at her. "You okay?"

"Sure." Tommi slammed her locker door shut. "It's just, you know, I'm kind of sick of talking about college, that's all."

"Okay." Zara wasn't sure where that had come from. As far as she was aware, they hadn't really been talking about college at all.

Before she could think about that, she heard someone calling Tommi's name. A moment later, her friend Duckface skidded to a stop in front of them. His strawberry-blond hair was sticking up in a way that would have looked ridiculous on anyone else, but somehow it almost worked on him. Zara glanced behind him, relieved to see that none of Tommi's boring female friends seemed to be following in his wake.

"Hey, ladies," Duckface said, sweeping into a dramatic bow in front of them. "How was the horse show? I kept checking Facebook for shots of you two in your tight riding pants holding your whips, but alas, I was denied."

Tommi rolled her eyes, but Zara laughed. "Perv," she said.

"That's my middle name." Duckface grinned. "Maybe we could grab a bite after school sometime, and I'll tell you all about it."

Zara hesitated. Even though Duckface was being goofy as usual, her guy radar—which rarely steered her wrong—was telling her the offer was real. And for once, she wasn't sure what to say. Okay, so Duckface wasn't exactly a male model, but Zara didn't care about that. She'd known too many externally hot guys out in LA who were about as much fun as a shoe full of horse manure. Give her an *interesting* guy any day. And Duckface was nothing if not interesting.

Still . . .

"Sorry." She kept her voice light. "I make it a habit never to be alone with waterfowl."

Duckface laughed so hard at the retort that he snorted, not seeming at all insulted or even particularly disappointed. Zara suspected it wasn't the first time he'd been shot down. Probably not even the first time today. He didn't seem like a guy who let much bother him.

So why did *she* feel bothered by the whole exchange? Maybe because there was no good reason she could pinpoint for turning him down, other than that her heart wasn't really in it?

Whatever. Since when did she need a better reason than that? Doing her best to shrug off her uneasy feelings, she told herself she was just too tired to deal right now. No biggie.

Pelham Lane was usually closed to clients on Mondays, but during Indoors season, the regular schedule went out the window. When Tommi pulled in after school, the parking lot was packed and she could see a few people taking advantage of the last few minutes of daylight in the outdoor rings.

Pocketing her keys, Tommi hurried inside. Marissa and Summer were sprawled on one of the benches in the entry area, phones in hand.

"Tommi!" Marissa immediately looked guilty when she raised her eyes. "Um, hi."

"What's going on?" Tommi's gaze shifted to Marissa's phone. "Wait, don't tell me—I'm in today's blog, right?"

"Maybe." Marissa smiled sheepishly and held out her phone. "It's just something about how you were seen hanging out with that cute Scott kid at Cap Challenge."

Summer's pale blue eyes glittered with interest. "Yeah, did you know his dad's some kind of computer tycoon? I heard Scott tried to buy some big-time Grand Prix jumper to do the high juniors with, but the owners turned him down even though he offered like a zillion bucks or something."

Tommi didn't bother to respond to that. Summer was always very interested in exactly how much money other people were spending, a habit Tommi found supremely irritating.

"At least the blog's somewhat accurate for once." Tommi handed Marissa's phone back. "Not that it's anyone's business who I hang out with. Least of all the entire Internet."

Marissa looked sympathetic. "I know, right?" she said. "I mean, I like a little gossip as much as the next girl . . ."

Tommi snorted, and even Summer shot Marissa a disbelieving look. Marissa giggled.

"Okay," she amended. "Maybe I like gossip even *more* than the next girl. My point is, the blogger's kind of out of control."

"Maybe." Summer shrugged. "But Zara says she's going to find out who's doing it."

Marissa stuck her phone in her pocket. "Do you really think she can figure it out?"

"Who knows?" Tommi had her doubts—Zara didn't exactly

have the world's longest attention span—but she was tired of discussing the blog. She glanced at her watch. "Hey, do you know if all the horses are in from turnout? I want to get on Orion, make sure we're ready to redeem ourselves in Harrisburg."

"I'm sure you will, Tommi," Summer said. "Everyone was totally surprised that you didn't win the eq at Cap Challenge, especially since Orion is so experienced at finals and all. But no big deal, right? It's not like anyone cares about that one— it's not even a real finals."

Tommi knew it was usually better to ignore Summer's more ignorant comments, but sometimes she just couldn't resist slapping her down. "You might not want to say that in front of the people who pinned," she told Summer, her voice coming out a little sharper than she meant it to. "They might not see it that way."

Summer's jaw dropped, and Tommi suspected that Marissa was trying not to giggle. "Um, I'm not sure about the horses being in from turnout," Marissa told Tommi quickly. "I think the guys are still bringing some of them in. Jamie wanted them out as long as possible to stretch their legs."

Tommi wasn't surprised to hear it. It had been a beautiful day, warm and breezy with practically no humidity, and she was sure the horses had enjoyed being out after more than a week in the cramped stalls at the show.

"Guess I'll go see," she said. "Catch you later."

She headed for Orion's stall. He wasn't there, so she continued out the back of the barn toward his usual turnout. When she reached the gate, he was grazing at the far end of the roomy paddock with his buddy, a placid older short-stirrup hunter named Scooby. At Tommi's whistle, both horses lifted their heads and started toward the gate—Scooby at a trot, and Orion at a dramatic hobble.

Tommi gasped. Yanking her phone out of her pocket, she texted Jamie and Joy:

Orion dead lame. Help!

"Easy, buddy," she said, grabbing a lead rope off the fence and slipping into the paddock as the horses reached the gate. Scooby nosed her, looking for treats, but she pushed his head away and went to Orion. "Let's see what's going on, okay?"

She slipped on his halter and shooed Scooby away. It was obvious that Orion was favoring his left front leg, so she ran her hand down it, feeling for heat or swelling. He lifted the hoof, leaving it hovering off the ground as Tommi squeezed and prodded gently. She was feeling around the hoof when she heard footsteps coming fast.

"Feel anything?" Joy asked breathlessly.

Tommi glanced up at the assistant trainer. "Hoof feels warm. He's not reacting when I poke anywhere else."

"Abscess then, probably." Joy came into the paddock and pushed Scooby away, bending to feel Orion's bad leg herself.

Tommi straightened up. "It's got to be, right?"

If her hands hadn't been busy, she would have crossed her fingers. An abscess—a localized infection inside the hoof—wasn't a *good* thing, exactly. But when a horse suddenly went lame, it was definitely the best of several possibilities. By far.

Just as Tommi glanced toward the barn, wondering how hard it was going to be to get Orion to walk there, she saw Jamie hurrying out the back door. "Got your message," he said when he reached the paddock.

"Thanks for coming so fast." Tommi bit her lip, watching as Joy's slim, tanned fingers continued to poke and prod. "I came out to get Orion, and he was practically three-legged."

"Yeah, looks like it's probably an abscess." Joy straightened up with a groan.

For a second, Tommi forgot about her horse. "You okay?" she asked Joy, flashing momentarily to all those rumors on the blog. Joy wasn't old enough to be groaning and complaining about her creaky old joints like Tommi's grandmother down in Florida. Tommi wasn't sure how old Joy was, actually, but it couldn't be much over thirty, if that.

"Sure. Just been a long day, that's all." Joy flashed her a smile. Was it Tommi's imagination, or did the woman look pale all of a sudden? "Anyway, let's get this guy into a stall, and I'll get the farrier out ASAP."

"Sounds like a plan." Jamie stepped in and grabbed Scooby. "Time for you to come in too, buddy."

Soon Orion was in his stall nosing at the pile of fresh-smelling hay one of the grooms had put in there. Joy pulled out her cell phone and wandered off down the aisle with it pressed to her ear while Tommi and Jamie stood watching the horse.

"Don't worry. Burt will have him feeling better in no time." Jamie glanced at her. "But you realize what this means, right?"

Tommi's heart sank. She'd been so anxious about Orion that she hadn't thought beyond trying to figure out what was behind his lameness. But now she realized what Jamie was saying. An abscess wasn't a serious problem, but it was serious enough to keep Orion home from the upcoming show.

"Yeah," she said, feeling her chances at Harrisburg's prestigious Medal Finals limping away. "Oh well, that's horses for you, I guess."

"All right, Kate." Ms. Chen handed Kate's English quiz back to her across her desk, an expression of mild concern on her face. "I realize Shakespeare can be challenging and you were away last week, but I'm concerned that if this happens again, your grade for the semester will suffer. Please ask for help next time if necessary, okay?"

"I will, I swear. Thanks." Kate grabbed the paper and shoved it into her bag, heading for the door before the teacher could change her mind.

That had been close. Kate had been so desperate to finish her chemistry homework on the drive home from Cap Challenge that she hadn't had time to finish reading *Macbeth*, and yesterday's quiz had taken her completely by surprise. Good thing her grades in English had been mostly decent otherwise this year. Because all it would take was one teacher calling Kate's parents before the trailers pulled out the next afternoon, and she could kiss Harrisburg good-bye.

She tried not to think about that. For one thing, she didn't have time. It was Tuesday afternoon, and the juniors had a lesson in a little over an hour. Before that, Kate was supposed to repack the tack stall drapes for the show, and there was a feed delivery scheduled that she might need to help organize. . . .

Kate was so busy listing off tasks in her head as she hurried across the student parking lot that she didn't notice anyone else was around until she heard a cough followed by Nat's nasally drawl: "In a hurry, Katie?"

Kate stopped short. Nat and Cody were sitting on the tailgate of his battered pickup, passing a bag of Doritos back and forth between them. The truck was parked right across from Kate's car, which was one of the last remaining in the lot.

"H-hi," Kate responded cautiously. She and Nat hadn't spoken since chemistry class the other week, and for a second Kate wondered if it was a good sign Nat was talking to her now. Was she finally starting to thaw?

Fat chance. "Let me guess." Nat popped a chip in her mouth and glared at Kate as she crunched. "You're rushing over to that fancy-schmancy snob barn of yours, right? Gotta hurry up and get there so the rich bitches can order you around."

Cody snorted with laughter. "Here's an order for you, Kate," he said. "Go get me a beer."

Nat ignored him, keeping her eyes trained on Kate's. "That where you're going, Katie?" she asked.

"It's not like that there—you know that, Nat," Kate blurted out, sidling a few steps closer to her car.

Nat shrugged. "While you're there, say hi to *my* horse, would ya?" she said. "Or wait. I guess you don't have to do what I say—you think you're better than me now, right? Only the rich bitches get to tell you what to do, and you just suck up to them and take it like some yappy little dog nobody really likes."

Kate didn't stick around to hear any more. She raced to her car, her hands shaking so badly she could barely get the key into the ignition. Finally jamming it in, she gunned the engine and took off without looking back.

She was still stewing over the confrontation with Nat when she arrived at Pelham Lane ten minutes later. Grabbing her well-worn paddock boots out of the backseat, she quickly yanked them on and hurried inside. Nobody was in the entry-way except one of the barn dogs, so Kate headed for the office to see if Jamie still wanted her to try to do the stall drapes before the lesson.

On her way, she passed the grooming stalls. Horses were cross-tied in several of them—Fitz's leased eq horse, Marissa's hunter, and Dani's jumper—though it looked as if their riders hadn't even started grooming yet, let alone tacking up.

Kate soon saw why. All three riders were huddled just down the aisle, along with Zara and Summer. The buzz of excited conversation drifted toward Kate. Was something going on?

Fitz looked up and spotted her. "She's here," he said loudly, which for some reason made the others fall silent.

"What's going on?" Kate took a few cautious steps toward the group. Zara waved at her, looking weirdly excited. Dani had a funny half smile on her face, and Marissa and Summer were staring at Kate as if she were the most fascinating thing they'd ever seen. Which was definitely *not* normal, especially for Summer, who rarely looked directly at Kate unless she was ordering her to do something. Sometimes not even then. For the ghost of a second, Nat's accusations darted back into Kate's mind, though she tried not to focus on them.

Fitz was already hurrying to meet her. "Hey," he said softly, bending to brush her lips with a quick kiss. "I guess you haven't heard yet, huh? Come on over here. You'll want to see this."

"See what?" She followed him back down the aisle. Zara held out her phone.

"Check it out," she said with a grin. "Guess this explains why Joy's been acting weird lately."

Kate blinked, not sure what she was talking about. Then she recalled Zara talking about the blog and Joy at Cap Challenge, though Kate had been too busy to do more than glance at it when Zara stuck it in front of her face at dinner one night.

"There's something about Joy on the blog again?" Kate said, taking the phone.

"Not just Joy." Fitz's arm slipped around her shoulders and squeezed. "Read it. All the way through."

Kate scanned the post:

> Your faithful blogger just uncovered some blockbuster news out of Pelham Lane Stables. Remember how assistant trainer Joy was acting funny? Well, now we know why—she's preggers! What does this mean for the future of PLS? Only head trainer Jamie Vos knows, and he's not saying—but odds seem good that he'll be looking for a new assistant very soon. Who will it be? Again, nobody knows for sure—but some say a certain working student will likely be asked to step into the job!

EIGHT

"What do you think?" Marissa asked Kate, her eyes shining with excitement.

Kate couldn't answer. Her mind felt numb, unable to process this.

Summer wrinkled her nose. "I think it's totally weird to picture Joy with a baby," she said. "I mean, I didn't even realize she was married."

"Yes, you did," Dani told her. "She brought her husband to the barn picnic last spring, remember? He's super shy and adorable. Works in real estate, I think."

"Not really the point here, guys." Fitz shot them an annoyed look. Then he turned to Kate. "Congratulations, babe," he said with a grin. "Should we call you Madame Trainer, or just Boss?"

Kate was still too stunned to respond, or even really take in what he'd said. She was still staring at the blog post on Zara's phone, trying to make sense of the words blinking at her from the tiny screen. Was Joy really leaving Pelham Lane? It was hard to imagine—she'd been there since long before Kate had arrived.

Even if that part was true, could the other part possibly be right? Could Jamie actually be thinking of offering Kate the more-than-full-time position of assistant trainer?

"This can't be for real," she blurted out at last. "I mean— it's crazy, right? I'm only sixteen."

"You'll be seventeen in a few months," Fitz reminded her.

"No, she's right," Summer said. "It's totally crazy. Kate can't be the assistant trainer."

"Why not?" Zara challenged her. "She rides better than anyone here except maybe Jamie."

"Yeah," Fitz agreed, giving Kate's shoulders an extra squeeze. "She'd be awesome at it. She practically runs this place as it is."

Just then Tommi rounded the corner leading Toccata. "What's going on?" she asked when she saw them all standing there.

Zara and the others practically tripped over themselves filling her in. Tommi's eyebrows shot higher with every word, and halfway through she grabbed the phone out of Kate's hand and scrolled through the blog post.

"This is nuts." She frowned at the screen. "I doubt it's more than some stupid rumor, like most of the other stuff on this blog." She handed Zara's phone back to her. "But even if Jamie goes temporarily insane and offers Kate the job, there's no way she'd accept it."

"Says who?" Fitz looked annoyed.

"Says anyone with half a brain." Tommi led her horse into an open grooming stall and clipped on the cross-ties as she talked. "I mean, think about it. She'd have to drop out of school, and college would be out of the question."

"That's true." Marissa glanced at Kate thoughtfully. "I hadn't really thought about it that way."

Zara shrugged. "Not everybody has to go to college. My dad didn't, and look where it got him."

Kate's mother hadn't gone to college, either, though she didn't bother to mention that. Since when was Tommi so gung-ho about college, anyway? Wasn't that the whole point of this horse-selling deal she had going with her father— that she didn't want to settle for being some generic college-bound drone? That she wanted to follow her dream of working with horses for a living? What made that okay for her but not for Kate?

Tommi was scowling at Zara and the others. "I'm just saying it's not realistic. And probably not even true."

Dani glanced at Kate. "You're being awfully quiet, Kate. What do you think? If it *is* true, would you take the job?"

Suddenly every eye was on Kate, making her feel like a butterfly in a jar. Her face was hot, and she wished she could be anywhere else. Why did that stupid blog have to write something like this, anyway? She had enough on her plate right now without one more thing—one more *big* thing—to worry about.

"Um . . . ," she began.

"Quiet!" Marissa hissed suddenly. "Jamie's coming."

Kate followed her gaze. The trainer had just rounded the corner. He frowned when he saw them.

"Why are you all standing around? Lesson starts in twenty minutes sharp." He glanced at the horses waiting more or less patiently in the grooming stalls nearby. "And it looks like some of you are going to have to hurry to be ready in time."

"Sorry, Jamie. We'll be ready," Marissa said, scurrying into the grooming bay, where her horse was dozing.

Jamie turned to Kate. "I was looking for you," he said. "Mind riding Mrs. Walsh's mare today instead of Fable? She was kind of a wreck at Cap Challenge, and could use another good schooling before she gets back on the trailer tomorrow."

"Sure. I'll go get her ready." Not quite meeting Jamie's eye, Kate took off down the aisle.

After the lesson, Tommi untacked as quickly as possible. Toccata hadn't put a hoof wrong, and Tommi was sure he'd be a superstar at Harrisburg. But it wasn't her hunter division she was thinking about as she returned the horse to his stall, fed him a peppermint, then headed toward the stable office. She'd had a brainstorm halfway through the lesson, and she needed to talk to Jamie about it right away if it was going to work out.

As she headed toward the office, she encountered Fitz and Marissa lounging in the aisle outside the tack room a couple of doors down. "Is Jamie in there?" Tommi asked them, nodding at the closed office door.

"Yeah." Marissa pursed her lips, shooting the door a meaningful glance. "He's with Joy."

Tommi swallowed a sigh. Were they still all worked up about that? Okay, so maybe it wasn't too hard to believe the part about Joy's pregnancy. That would actually explain a lot about the assistant trainer's behavior lately. But could anyone seriously think Jamie would offer her job to a teenager—even one as responsible, hardworking, and talented as Kate?

Fitz seemed to guess what Tommi was thinking. "It could be true, you know," he said, sounding a little defensive. "Kate could do the job. I'm sure Jamie knows it. He'd be a fool not to consider her."

"Okay, fine." Tommi wasn't going to argue. Let them believe some crazy Internet rumor if they wanted. She just hoped Kate had enough sense not to fall for the story.

Tommi's phone buzzed, and she dug it out of her pocket. "Hot date?" Fitz teased.

Tommi glanced at the screen. "It's my friend Abby. You guys probably know her—she goes to Kirk with you."

"Sure, everyone knows Abby." Fitz nodded. "She's cool."

"Yeah, she's in a couple of my classes." Suddenly Marissa looked worried. "She's not saying anything about a math quiz, is she?"

"Nope." Tommi scanned the text. "She's all excited because she just sent off her application to Stanford."

"Already?" Fitz raised an eyebrow.

"She's applying early action. It's her first choice. And yeah, it's still early—Abs comes across as laid-back, but she can be a little type A about some stuff. "

Even via text, Abby sounded really excited—she wanted Tommi and their other friends to meet up with her right now to celebrate. Tommi quickly texted back that she was out at the barn and couldn't make it.

"Early action? Oh good." Marissa looked relieved. "I've

barely started my apps—my mom was harassing me about it just yesterday. She's afraid I'll run out of time 'cause I'm so busy with Indoors."

"Where are you applying?" Fitz asked. "Don't forget, my dad said he'd write you a rec for Colgate if you decide to apply."

"I know, and thanks, that's amazing." Marissa grimaced. "I'm afraid it might take more than that to get me in there, though."

"Hey, you won't know unless you go for it," Fitz said. "What have you got to lose?"

"You're right. I'll probably apply and cross my fingers." Marissa smiled. "I heard they have an amazing art history department. And that the people there are really nice."

Fitz nodded. "My dad loved it. He's making me apply, even though I'm pretty sure it's not going to be my first choice."

There was more, but Tommi stopped listening. Marissa was always enthusiastic about everything she did, but even Fitz sounded weirdly geeked about the whole applying-to-college thing. So did Abby, when she talked about Stanford, and Court when she sorted and re-sorted the list of schools she wanted to apply to, and most of Tommi's other senior friends, too. Even Duckface—crazy, life-of-the-party, devil-may-care Duckface, for god's sake—was all about getting into Yale these days.

Tommi just didn't get it. They all seemed so eager to move on all of a sudden. Their lives would be so totally different this time next year—why rush it? What was the big hurry for things to change?

She closed her eyes, hating the unsettled feeling the whole

topic gave her whenever she let herself think about it. It was like time was moving too fast and too slowly at the same time—and worse yet, there was nothing Tommi could do about it.

"What about you?" Marissa asked, breaking into Tommi's thoughts. "I don't think I've even asked where you're applying."

"Let me guess—the old man's probably making you apply to Georgetown, right?" Fitz grinned and elbowed Tommi.

She smiled weakly. "I haven't really narrowed it down yet. I'm mostly focused on Indoors right now, and finding another project to train up."

That was true, mostly. Tommi didn't like to admit it, even to herself, but sometimes she wondered—what if she couldn't make things work in the horse business? Everyone was always saying how hard it was, and Tommi had really only made one successful transaction so far. What if the next horse she tried to flip was a dud, or colicked right before the sale went through? What if she never found that second horse at all?

Maybe Tommi's father wasn't all wrong when he said she should consider all her options. Maybe she needed to think about what her future might look like just in case her horse business didn't pan out . . .

At that moment the office door swung open. Joy hurried out, holding a clipboard. "Hi, guys," she greeted Tommi and the others. "Looking for Jamie? He's inside."

"Great." Tommi stepped toward the door. Then she paused and glanced at Fitz and Marissa. "You guys weren't waiting for Jamie too, were you?"

"Nope, he's all yours," Fitz said as Marissa waved Tommi on.

"Thanks." Pushing all thoughts of college applications, horse flipping, and assistant trainer jobs out of her mind, Tommi hurried into the office. Jamie was bent over some paperwork on his desk.

He glanced up. "Hi, Tommi. What's up?"

Tommi took a deep breath. "I was thinking about something during the lesson today, and I had an idea I wanted to run past you."

NINE

— — — — —

"Sure you don't want to come, Little Z?" Zara's father asked as he wandered across the loft, leaving a spicy scent cloud of aftershave in his wake. "Heard this place has the best sushi in New York."

"Nah." Zara stuck her pen in her mouth, studying the Spanish workbook on the coffee table in front of her. A stack of other schoolbooks sat nearby, along with Zara's laptop and a big cup of coffee. "I'd better stay here and study."

Her mother had been applying lipstick in the mirrored foyer wall, but she stopped short and turned around at Zara's words. "Did I hear that right?" Gina said. "You're turning down a night out to *study*?" She hustled over and pressed the back of one perfectly manicured hand to Zara's forehead. "Doesn't feel like you're running a fever."

Zara pushed her mother's hand away. "Very funny. Hey, you're always ragging on me about keeping my grades up, right? Besides, if I have to watch you two do your usual date-night drool thing, I won't be able to eat anyway."

Zac chuckled and stepped over to plant a big, sloppy kiss on his wife's lips. "Stop!" Gina protested. "You're smearing my lipstick."

Zara rolled her eyes. Ever since Gina had finished her location shoot and Zac had returned from his European tour, the two of them had been making a point to go out on the town together as often as possible, often resulting in various paparazzi shots appearing in the papers the next day of the two of them smooching at yet another trendy restaurant or nightclub. It was totally gross, but at least it got them both out of the apartment at the same time.

"Just go already," Zara said. "You're distracting me, and I have a test on this stuff tomorrow."

"All right, my love." Gina bent and brushed her lips over Zara's cheek. "Come on, Zac. I'll redo my lipstick in the car."

Moments later they were gone. Zara waited until she heard the muffled clank of the elevator arriving, then pushed her Spanish book away. She stood, stretched, and walked over to the wall of windows. It was around seven thirty, and there were quite a few people out and about along with the usual amount of traffic. Still, Zara immediately spotted the limo idling at the curb below, and after a moment she saw her parents emerge from the building. A man walking his dog stopped to stare as Mickey opened the car door to usher Zac and Gina in, but nobody else even slowed down. That was one good thing about their SoHo neighborhood. Most of the people who lived there were too cool to gawk at celebrities. Or at least they liked to act as if they were, which was good enough.

Zara watched the limo pull away and then turn to join the

traffic going past on Broome Street. As soon as the car was out of sight, she hurried back to the sofa, grabbed her laptop, and flipped it open. She quickly pulled up HorseShowSecrets and scanned the latest entry—some boring gossip about a junior rider at a barn in North Carolina. Normally Zara wouldn't give it a second glance, since she didn't know the people involved and had never even set foot in North Carolina. But this time she studied it carefully before scrolling back to the previous post, and then the one before that.

"Who could know about all this stuff?" she muttered under her breath. "There's got to be a clue here somewhere."

Grabbing her Spanish notebook, she flipped to one of the blank pages in the back. Scrolling back to the top of the blog postings, she started going through them again, jotting down how many times each barn appeared. Maybe that would help her narrow down what region the blogger was from, anyway. Of course, the fact that most of the A circuit had been at Cap Challenge last week might make that harder. . . .

Her phone buzzed, and Zara scrabbled through the papers on the coffee table until she found it. "Hello?" she blurted out, not even bothering to check who was calling.

"Zara? That you?"

It was a male voice, but Zara didn't recognize it. She finally glanced at the screen, which identified the caller as Hersh Feldman. Who?

"Um, yeah, it's me," she said. "Who's this?"

"Hersh?" the guy said. "We met at that record company party last month, remember?"

"Oh right." Now Zara *did* remember, at least vaguely.

The party had been pretty boring, but Zara had entertained herself by flirting with the cute son of one of Zac's session musicians. "How's it going?"

"Good." The guy cleared his throat. "Listen, you doing anything this weekend? Because this friend of mine is having a party at this really cool club downtown, and I thought maybe you'd want to check it out."

"Sorry, no can do." Zara switched the phone to her other ear so she could scroll through the blog as she talked. "I'm going to be out of town at a horse show."

"Oh. Too bad." The guy sounded bummed. "Maybe some other time, huh?"

"Sure, maybe. Later." Zara hung up and stared at the phone. Something was bothering her, but she couldn't put her finger on what it was. It definitely wasn't because she'd turned down some random date. For one thing, she really was going to be away—all the juniors were riding down to Harrisburg together tomorrow night. And it wasn't as if she went out with every guy who asked, anyway.

So what then? She scrolled absently through the old messages on her phone, trying to figure it out. She blinked, her thumb frozen over the button as one name popped into view.

Marcus.

Okay, *now* she got the connection. Sort of. Marcus was another guy she'd met at one of her parents' functions, another guy who'd asked her out afterward. Was she really still thinking about him? Because there wasn't much point.

Her face went hot as she recalled how things had ended between them. That stupid blog had been responsible, actually. At least mostly. Zara had misinterpreted something Marcus had said to her, which had led to her accusing him of being behind the blog. As it turned out, he didn't even know about it and had been totally offended, and Zara hadn't heard from him since.

So what, though? Why had some random call from some random guy reminded her of *that*? The whole thing with Marcus shouldn't still be bothering her. Like, at all. She'd never let one guy—especially one she'd only gone out with for about three hot seconds—mess her up like that. No way.

She frowned and tossed her phone aside, pulling the laptop closer. At least thinking about that whole stupid scene with Marcus had done one good thing. It made her more determined than ever to figure out who *was* behind that freaking blog.

"Steady," Kate murmured as she rode Flame around the short side of the indoor ring. His trot felt round and collected under her. When they came out of the corner, she closed her legs softly, asking him to lengthen. For a second he tensed, but then he seemed to figure out what she was asking and his long legs stretched out smoothly, eating up the ground.

Kate smiled. She'd been afraid that Flame might forget everything she'd taught him while she was away at Cap Challenge. But if anything, he'd felt better than ever this week. Of course, it wasn't as if he'd been sitting around in his stall the whole time she was gone. Joy had promised to school him at least every other day or so.

Thinking about Joy made Kate's whole body tense up. The horse felt it, and his stride faltered, one ear flicking back toward Kate.

"Easy, buddy," Kate whispered, asking for a downward

transition and then giving him a pat. "It's okay. Sorry I got distracted."

She blew out a sigh, glancing around the empty ring. It was late, probably after nine. Kate wasn't sure exactly, since she'd taken off her watch before bathing a pony in the wash stall earlier and forgotten to put it back on. The barn had been even busier than usual, since everyone was rushing to get ready to leave for Harrisburg the next afternoon. After the juniors' lesson, Kate had been so busy she'd barely had time to breathe, let alone think about that blog entry.

Now, in the hushed dimness of the indoor, it came creeping back. Could it be true? Kate had dreamed of a career in horses since she was old enough to know what a horse was. For the past two and a half years she'd spent all her spare time and then some right here working toward that goal.

Even so, the very idea of taking over Joy's job seemed unreal. Impossible. Something that might happen in a movie or something. Not in real life, not to a girl like her. No way.

Flame stopped suddenly and lowered his head, rubbing his nose against his knee and making the bit jingle. Kate realized she'd been riding along like a lump of clay, just sitting there and letting the horse amble at his own pace. Some trainer she was . . .

Smiling ruefully, she gathered up the reins and clucked, sending the horse into a marching walk and then after a moment asking for the left-lead canter. Flame stepped effortlessly into the gait. For a moment Kate felt his energy build, but a half-halt reminded the horse that this was not the racetrack. He settled immediately, his stride smooth and steady as they rounded the next turn.

Kate floated along in half seat, enjoying the ride. She couldn't wait to see what Flame would do in the show ring someday. It was easy to imagine away the quiet Pelham Lane indoor and pretend that the two of them were cantering softly around the turn to a big square oxer at Harrisburg. . . .

For a second the vision shifted, and instead of Flame, Kate imagined herself aboard that fancy hunter belonging to Kara Parodi's client. She'd been too busy to think much about that, either, though she knew she'd have to figure out what to do soon. Tommi and Zara both seemed to think she should do it, that it was nothing out of the ordinary and Jamie wouldn't mind a bit, and for a while Kate had started to believe them. What was the big deal? She'd almost made up her mind to mention it to Jamie the next time she got a chance.

Now, though, that blog post had made everything much more complicated. How could she ask him about riding for a competitor? Would something like that change his mind, make him wonder if she was loyal enough to be his assistant?

Kate sat back and brought Flame down to a walk. Giving the horse a pat, she was about to turn across the diagonal when she caught a flash of movement by the gate. It was Fitz. He raised a hand and smiled, his face shadowy in the dimness outside the reach of the overhead lights.

"Hi," Kate said, riding over. "I didn't see you there."

"I've only been here a few minutes." Fitz patted Flame as the horse reached over the fence to nose at him. "Didn't want to interrupt. You guys look gorgeous out there—both of you."

"Thanks." Kate gave Flame a scratch on the withers. "He's really coming along."

"I can see that." Fitz watched the horse. "Think he'll be ready to show by the time we leave for Florida?"

"Um . . ." Kate wasn't sure how to respond. Much of Pelham Lane packed up and traveled to Florida every year for the big winter circuit down there. Kate had never gone—for the past two years she'd stayed behind to help Joy take care of things at home. Kate was hoping that if Indoors went well and she could convince her parents and teachers she wouldn't flunk out, maybe they'd let her go to Florida this year. But there was no guarantee they'd go for it. In fact, she was pretty much assuming she'd be left behind this year as usual.

Fitz noticed her hesitation. "Oh, wait," he said. "I almost forgot. If you take that assistant trainer job, I guess you'll have to stay home and teach lessons and stuff." He frowned and chewed his lower lip, glancing at Flame. "Oh well. We can always bring him out at one of the local shows in the spring. Or maybe you can fly down for the weekend and hop on."

Kate didn't bother to remind him that she couldn't afford a plane ticket to Florida. He would only offer to pay for it, and that kind of thing always made her uncomfortable.

"Nobody's offering me a job yet," she said instead.

Fitz leaned on the ring fence. "I know. But you saw that blog. Why would someone make up a story like that if there wasn't at least a grain of truth to it?"

Kate shrugged, picking at a scrap of hay caught in Flame's mane. "People make stuff up all the time," she said softly, thinking of some of the rumors Nat had started over the past couple of months. Like that Kate was on probation for dealing drugs, and the only reason nobody knew about it was that her police officer father had hushed it up. Or that she was sleeping with every guy in school. Or worse, that she was sleeping with Jamie, and that was why she was allowed to ride at Pelham Lane. Which was crazy, of course—Jamie didn't even like girls. But Nat had never let the facts stand in the way of a good smear campaign. Kate knew that. And now she knew how it felt to have the full force of Nat's wrath turned against her.

"What?" Fitz reached over and poked Kate's leg just above the top of her half chaps. "You're a million miles away all of a sudden. Thinking about how awesome you'd be at that job?"

"Not exactly." Kate's gaze skittered toward him, then away. "I mean, you heard what Tommi said earlier. I'd have to drop out of school. My parents would never go for that."

"It's your life, not your parents'." Fitz's hand was still on her knee, and he squeezed gently. "But listen, don't let it stress you out, okay? You should talk to Jamie, see if you can work something out. Maybe he'd let you do the job part time so you can stay in school. Or maybe you can do some kind of home-schooling thing—you could do your schoolwork online at night after you get home from the barn, or maybe your mom could teach you or something."

Kate bit her lip, still playing with Flame's mane. "I don't think any of those things will work."

"Why not?"

Kate could list at least a dozen reasons why not, but she didn't bother. Sometimes things that were obvious to her seemed completely foreign to Fitz, and vice versa. He came from a world where everything pretty much *did* work out, while in Kate's world that definitely wasn't a guarantee. Not even close.

"Anyway, I'm *not* saying anything to Jamie," she told him. "You shouldn't either, okay? I mean, what if none of it's true? I'd look like an idiot."

Fitz just shrugged. "Okay, I'll keep my mouth shut." he said. "But you know I'm here for you, no matter what happens."

"Thanks." That actually made Kate feel better, at least a little. Who could have guessed that Fitz would turn out to be the most steady and reliable part of her life?

Fitz glanced at his watch. "You almost finished with your ride? Because I want to take you to dinner in the city."

Kate was still thinking about the job, but now she blinked, wondering if she'd heard him wrong. "Dinner? What, tonight?"

"Yeah, tonight. It's our last night here, remember?" He grinned. "I thought we could use a last hurrah before the craziness of Indoors gears up again tomorrow."

"Oh." Kate realized the two of them hadn't been out on a real date since before Capital Challenge. There just hadn't been time. Unfortunately, there really wasn't time now, either. "Um, that sounds nice. But it's getting late, and I've still got a half day of school tomorrow."

"Come on." Fitz blinked up at her with that puppy-dog gaze she found almost impossible to resist, his fingers tiptoeing up her leg. "I need my Kate fix. We'll make it quick, I swear."

Kate was tempted to give in and say yes. She could use a break, especially with another solid week of hard work and no sleep coming up. But even the thought of the long drive down to Manhattan made her want to yawn.

"Sorry," she said reluctantly. "I really can't. I need to finish my English paper tonight, and I should get started on some of my other homework too. Besides, my dad will flip out if I'm not home before his shift ends at midnight."

Fitz pursed his lips. "Okay, how's this," he said. "No city. Just dinner. Finish up and we can hit the diner, and I'll have you home by eleven thirty. Promise. What do you say?"

Kate hesitated. She really did need to get on that homework, and she'd planned to try to get to sleep early, since it would definitely be a late night tomorrow by the time the barn finished setting up and settling in at the show. Then again, the diner was only a few miles away, and she *did* have to eat.

"Sure, sounds good," she said before she could overthink it any more. "Just let me finish up with Flame, and we can go."

"Awesome." Fitz grinned and stepped back. "I'll help you untack and put him away."

Kate nodded, trying not to calculate how late she would probably be up finishing that English paper. Sleep was over-rated, right?

Then again, maybe she shouldn't lose sleep over some stupid essay on *Macbeth*. If she got that assistant trainer job, none of that stuff would matter anymore—she'd never have to read Shakespeare again if she didn't want to, or learn any of the other useless stuff she was studying in school. The thought made her smile as she nudged Flame into motion.

TEN

By the time she reached the barn on Wednesday, Tommi was feeling seriously tense. It didn't help that Zara had chattered nonstop through the whole long drive up from Manhattan, seeming as giddy as an elementary school kid at getting out of school after a half day. She'd mostly talked about her investigation into the source of that blog, at least as far as Tommi could tell. She'd stopped listening around the time they'd hit the Triborough.

She pulled into one of the spots in the corner of the parking area, where her car would be out of the way during the week. Then she popped the trunk.

"Grab your stuff," she told Zara. "I want to lock up and drop my keys in the office in case Joy needs to move my car while we're gone."

"Aye aye, captain." Zara performed what was probably supposed to be a salute, though it looked more like some kind of warped disco move. Hoisting her bags out of the trunk, she hurried off toward the barn.

Tommi followed more slowly, her anxiety building. There was something she needed to do before everyone hit the road to Harrisburg in a few hours, and she wasn't looking forward to it.

When she walked into the barn, Zara was huddled with Marissa and Dani. The three of them abruptly stopped talking when Tommi came in, then laughed with relief.

"Oh, it's just you." Marissa smiled at Tommi. "We don't want Jamie or Joy or any of the other adults to hear what we're saying. For obvious reasons." Her gaze fell to the cell phone in Dani's hand.

"Right," Tommi muttered. She didn't have time for this right now. "Have you guys seen Kate?"

"I think she's finishing up with the last of the baths." Dani gestured in the general direction of the wash stalls, then nodded toward a pile of suitcases and other gear near the door. "By the way, you can put your stuff there. Miguel's going to bring the van up and load everything in a bit."

Tommi did as she said, adding her bags to the pile of luggage. Then she headed down the aisle toward the wash stall area.

Kate was rinsing the suds off a stout pinto pony. "Hey," she greeted Tommi breathlessly. "You made it. We're running a little late. But Jamie thinks we can start loading the horses in about an hour or so."

"Cool." Tommi glanced around to make sure they were alone. "Listen, can I talk to you about something?"

Kate grabbed a towel and dried her hands. "Sure. What is it?"

Tommi took a deep breath, forcing herself to meet Kate's

eye. They were friends; she didn't deserve any less. "It's about Fable."

"Fable?" Kate looked confused. "What about him?"

"You know Orion's out of action for Harrisburg, right?"

Kate nodded, her blue eyes sympathetic. "Timing sucks. At least you'll probably only have to miss the one finals, right?"

"That's the thing," Tommi said. "I worked hard to qualify, and I really didn't want to miss this one. So I arranged with Jamie to, uh, to lease Fable for Harrisburg."

Kate's jaw dropped. "What? Um, I mean, wow. I didn't hear about that."

"It only got finalized last night." Tommi watched Kate carefully. "You okay? I would have talked to you about it first, but with the timing . . ."

"No, forget it, it's fine. It's not like you need my permission or whatever." Kate grabbed a sweat scraper and went to work on the pony, scraping the moisture from its clean coat. "I was just surprised, that's all. But I'm glad it worked out."

"Really?" Relief flooded through Tommi's body. "Awesome. I was afraid you might . . . Well, I just know how hard you've been working with Fable these past few months. He wouldn't be ready to do an eq final if it wasn't for you."

Kate glanced at Tommi over her shoulder. "He's a cool horse. You know that—you rode him a few times at the beginning of the summer, right?"

"Yeah. That reminds me." Tommi checked her watch. "It's been a while since I've been on him. I was hoping there might be time to hop on and take him for a quick spin before we leave. What do you think? Is it worth asking Jamie?"

Kate nodded. "Like I said, it'll be at least an hour before the guys bring the trailers up. I'm not sure where Jamie is, but you could text him."

Moments later it was settled. Jamie called back and gave permission for Tommi to squeeze in a short ride on Fable. "It'll probably be good for him," the trainer said, sounding distracted. "Take the edge off, since he's just been sitting around eating for most of the past two weeks."

Tommi thanked him and hung up. Kate was watching her.

"If you want . . . ," Kate began, then hesitated. "I mean, I just have to finish with this pony, and then I should have a few minutes free. I could come give you some pointers. Not that you need them, but you know . . ."

"That would be amazing." Tommi smiled. "You probably know Fable better than anyone at this point. Meet you in the indoor in ten?"

"See you there."

"Thanks, Kate." Tommi hurried off, feeling a million times calmer than she had a few minutes earlier.

Twenty minutes later, Kate stood in the center of the ring and watched as Tommi trotted Fable around her. There was only one other rider in the indoor, an older adult rider who didn't attend the fall shows. She was working on small figure eights at the far end, leaving most of the ring for Tommi. That was a good thing, since Fable was full of energy and didn't mind letting his rider know it. He blew through an obvious half-halt, bounding from the trot into an exuberant canter.

"Don't be afraid to be firm with him," Kate called out. "He likes to test you, but he'll listen if you convince him it's worth his while."

"Got it." Tommi's expression was focused and determined as she half-halted again. This time Fable responded well, coming back to trot and rounding up.

"Nice!" Kate called. "That looks great."

She wasn't surprised that Tommi was already getting the hang of the big gray gelding. Even though some people seemed to believe that Tommi had bought her way to success in the show ring, Kate knew better. Her friend was talented, brave, and always working hard to become a better rider. She rode anything Jamie offered her, never complaining if a horse had quirks or needed reschooling. She deserved to show that off at Medal Finals instead of having to sit it out. It would be good experience for Fable to compete in one of the big, prestigious finals, too.

Kate bit her lip, trying to ignore the tiny voice bubbling up inside her, reminding her that *she* was supposed to be the one to give Fable that experience. She was the one who'd worked with him all summer, teaching him what he needed to know, fighting his stubborn streak through countless lessons, riding him to an increasing number of ribbons at the shows. . . .

She tamped down those feelings as best she could. It didn't matter. Kate hadn't qualified for finals. She'd started too late in the season, the horse had been too green at the beginning, and there had been no time or money for last-minute point chasing at the end. Meanwhile, Tommi was qualified and thus able to ride any horse she wanted in the finals. End of story. Kate should be happy for her friend, not resentful or upset.

"Loosen up on your outside rein a little," she called out as Tommi trotted past again. "Let him carry himself. That'll tell you he's ready to go to work."

Tommi nodded, doing as Kate suggested. After that, she proceeded to canter and even popped over a few fences. When she pulled up a few minutes later, Tommi was smiling.

"Thanks for talking me through that," she said. "I feel pretty good about this now."

"You look pretty good. Great, actually." That was true. And Kate was happy for her friend. Really.

So why did she feel so weird about this?

"Knock knock!" Without waiting for a response, Dani burst through the open door to Zara's hotel room. "What are you doing?"

Zara hit mute on the TV remote. It was a little after nine thirty on Wednesday evening, and the entire barn had come back from dinner about half an hour earlier.

"Nothing," Zara said. "You look happy. Are you drunk? And if so, are you planning to share or what?"

Dani giggled. "Not drunk, just psyched to be back at the shows." She flung herself onto Zara's bed. "I was bored out of my skull while you guys were at Cap Challenge."

"So we should celebrate your triumphant return." Zara grinned. "Party in your room?"

"Funny you should mention parties." Dani rolled over onto her back, smiling up at Zara. "I was just hanging out with some friends from Top Meadows—"

"Where?"

Dani laughed again. "Right, I forgot you're still new to the East Coast scene. Top Meadows is this barn in South Jersey. You know that really pretty girl with the Celtic horse tattoo on her wrist? She rides there."

Zara had no clue what girl Dani was talking about, but that didn't seem important. "So?" she prompted.

"So Jane heard one of the guy riders from Fordleigh—that's this other barn in New Jersey—is throwing a party in his room to help kick off junior weekend."

Junior weekend was the reason they were all there. It started the next day and consisted of three straight days of junior hunter and pony divisions, followed by the Hunter Seat Equitation Medal Finals on Sunday. Zara tossed the remote aside. "So what are we waiting for? Hang on, I need to find my shoes."

Soon Zara and Dani were hurrying down the hall. "Which room is Tommi in again? Is it number eight or nine?" Dani paused, glancing from one closed door to the other.

"Nine, I think." Zara raised her hand to knock.

Dani grabbed it. "Wait!" she hissed with a nervous giggle. "Are you sure? We don't want to knock on, like, Jamie's door by mistake, or some random person!"

"What, you're afraid to live dangerously?" Zara shook her hand free and pretended she was going to knock on the door anyway, then pulled back and dug her phone out of her pocket. "Okay, we'll play it safe."

She texted Tommi. A few seconds later one of the doors opened.

"See?" Zara told Dani. "I was right."

"What's going on?" Tommi asked.

"Party," Zara replied. "You in?"

Tommi glanced at her watch and shrugged. "Sure, I guess. Probably won't stay late, though—I want to get over to the show early and work with Fable."

"We'll see." Zara grabbed her arm and dragged her out into the hall.

"Wait!" Tommi protested. "Give me a minute to change— I'm not going like this."

Belatedly, Zara noticed that Tommi was dressed in flannel pajama pants and slippers. "Fine, but hurry up."

"It's room thirty-seven," Dani told Tommi. "We'll meet you there."

As Tommi nodded and disappeared back into her room, Zara glanced at Dani. "Who else should we invite? Where's Marissa?"

"Doing her makeup," Dani said. "I'll hurry her along if you go try to talk to Kate."

"Kate?" Zara was surprised. "I assumed she'd be back at the show, like, tucking the horses in or whatever."

Dani shook her head. "She's in our room, studying. I tried to convince her to come, but she wasn't into it. Maybe you can change her mind."

Zara nodded. Kate and Dani often shared rooms at shows to save money, though sometimes Zara wondered why Kate bothered getting a hotel room at all, since she seemed to spend about twenty-three and a half hours a day at the show working.

"I'll see what I can do," Zara told Dani. "What's your room number?"

Soon she was knocking on another door. "It's open!" Kate called from inside.

When Zara entered, Kate was sitting in the middle of one of the double beds, books and papers spread out around her. She looked stressed, but then that was nothing new. As far as Zara could tell, the girl lived in a constant state of stress.

"Hey, didn't you hear?" Zara stepped over and flipped Kate's textbook shut. "No studying allowed after nine p.m. It's, like, a Pennsylvania state law or something."

Kate didn't look amused. "Stop," she said, flipping through the book. "I really want to finish these problem sets."

"They'll wait till tomorrow. We've got a party to go to!"

"Sorry." Kate found her page and huddled over the book. "I already told Dani I can't go."

"Says who?" Zara said. "Your math teacher isn't here, and neither are your parents. Nobody's going to tattle if you sneak off to have fun for five minutes. So come on—live a little!"

Kate glanced up with a frown. "Easy for you to say," she snapped. "If I ever want to go to another show, I need to keep my grades up."

Zara raised both eyebrows, startled by the bite in Kate's voice. *So* not like her. Usually the girl was too nice and polite for her own good.

"Whoa," Zara said. "Sorry, I was just kidding around. But seriously, what's the big deal? You've got all week to study."

"Not really." Kate shook her head. "I mean, I'm still behind from Cap Challenge, and if I don't catch up by the time we get back, my teachers are going to start calling my parents."

"Yeah?" Zara still didn't get it. "So they'll understand, right? Indoors only happens once a year, and it's a big deal."

"Not to my parents," Kate countered. "It's practically a miracle they even let me come to this one. All they need is an excuse, any excuse at all, and they'll make me skip the rest of the shows."

"Wow." If someone like Marissa or Dani or even Tommi had said the exact same thing, Zara would have assumed she was exaggerating. Kate could be sort of melodramatic at times, but Zara could tell that this time, she was deadly serious. "So your parents are pretty hardcore, huh?"

"They think school is, like, super important." Kate played with the corner of her textbook, her long blond hair falling forward to hide her face. "They don't get the horse thing at all."

"Gotcha." Zara flopped down on the bed next to her. "Then listen, it's lucky you know me. I'm probably the world's number-one expert at hiding bad grades—and all kinds of other stuff—from parents. I can help you."

Kate looked dubious. "You can?"

"Sure. This one time a couple of years ago I was totally flunking out of math class, and I managed to keep my parents from ever finding out."

"Really? How'd you do that?"

Zara shrugged. "Well, my dad was easy. He was touring in Australia at the time," she said. "And of course I just deleted all the e-mails my teacher sent before my parents could get them."

"Of course." Kate looked a little shocked.

"Yeah," Zara said. "And luckily this happened right when all the Oscar buzz was starting up, and I told my mom I overheard some people saying she was a shoo-in for Best Supporting Actress for some dumb-ass spy thriller she had out that year. She forgot I existed for the next two or three weeks, and by then I'd brought the grade up again."

Kate smiled faintly. "Um, I don't think the Oscar-buzz thing is going to work on my parents."

"Good point." Zara rubbed her chin. "Okay, then there was the time I should've gotten in huge trouble for appearing in this skanky tabloid in, let's just say, not as many clothes as I should've had on."

This time Kate actually laughed. "Wow," she said. "Um, I'm thinking I wouldn't have to worry about that one, because if my parents saw something like that they'd both have heart attacks and die."

Kate actually looked a bit more cheerful. Zara grinned. Hey, at least her wild-child past was good for something.

Zara had left the door ajar when she entered. Now it swung open and Fitz peeked in. "Hey," he said. "Everybody decent in there?"

"No, but it's cool. Come on in," Zara called.

She saw Kate look over at Fitz, her whole face sort of lighting up when she saw him. Cute.

"Did you guys hear about the party in thirty-seven?" Fitz hurried in and dropped a kiss on top of Kate's head.

"Yeah. I was just trying to talk your girlfriend into going," Zara said. "She's not buying it from me, but maybe your hunky manliness will change her mind."

Fitz grinned and flexed. "I'll try," he said in a fake deep voice.

Kate laughed. "Seriously, you guys." She brushed her hair out of her face. "I should study."

She didn't sound quite as convinced as before. Zara glanced at Fitz. "You grab her left arm, I've got the other one."

"Cool." Fitz caught Kate by the wrist and tugged gently.

"Come on, gorgeous. We'll just go for a little while, and if it's lame, we'll leave."

"But . . ." Kate hesitated, glancing at her schoolbooks.

Zara gave a yank on Kate's arm. "We're not taking no for an answer," she said. "Look, would it help if I promised to help with your homework tomorrow?"

"You?" Fitz looked skeptical. "Um, last I heard you weren't exactly an academic superstar."

Zara stuck out her tongue at him. "Says who? I could be a genius if I wanted to."

Kate laughed, finally allowing them to pull her off the bed. "Fine, shut up, I'll go. But only for a few minutes."

Zara grinned triumphantly. "Awesome! Now hurry, let's get up there before Dani drinks all the beer."

ELEVEN

An hour later, the party was in full swing. Tommi had found herself a seat on the AC unit under the window, where she was listening without much interest as Marissa and some girl from Ohio whose name she'd forgotten argued over some stupid TV show Tommi had never seen. The hotel room was stuffy and overly warm, laced with the scents of sweat and beer. People were crammed into every corner of the place—it seemed as if every junior attending Harrisburg had turned up. A guy was digging through the minibar, tossing tiny bottles of alcohol, cans of soda, and bags of peanuts at any cute girl who walked past. A couple was making out on one of the beds as if they were the only ones in the room. Several girls were dancing on the other bed, occasionally falling off to raucous laughter. The music was loud enough that Tommi couldn't believe the other hotel guests hadn't complained yet.

"This is great, isn't it?" Marissa shouted into her ear.

Tommi forced a smile. "Sure," she said. "But I think I should—"

Marissa had already turned away to shout something at the other girl. A second later she jumped to her feet.

"Need another beer?" she asked Tommi.

Tommi shook her head and held up her bottle, which was still at least two-thirds full. She wasn't in the mood for getting drunk tonight. Not with the Large Juniors starting tomorrow. For some reason Toccata always seemed to find the ring at Harrisburg particularly distracting, and Tommi would need to be on her toes. Besides that, she meant what she'd said about wanting to get on Fable early. Her test ride that afternoon had gone pretty well, but "pretty well" wouldn't take her far in the eq finals. If she was going to compete, she wanted to be ready to do her best.

The girl from Ohio was chattering to some guy who'd just wandered over. Marissa danced off toward the bathroom, where beer was chilling in the tub. Left alone, Tommi sneaked a peek at her watch, thinking about calling it a night.

She glanced at the door, trying to estimate the best path through the hordes of partying juniors. At that moment it swung open and three more people came in. One of them was Scott Papadakis.

Suddenly Tommi felt a lot more interested in the party. She watched as Scott traded high fives with a few of the other partiers and stopped to chat with a cluster of girls near the TV. Halfway to the bathroom door, he noticed Tommi watching him.

He stopped short and leaned over to say something to his friends. They both turned and stared at Tommi with interest. Then Scott peeled off and came toward her.

"Hey," he said when he reached her. "What's up, Tommi?"

"Not much." She took a sip of her beer. "Quite a party, huh?"

"Yeah." He grinned and glanced around. "Hard to believe half of these people have to be on a horse at, like, eight a.m. for the Small Juniors."

Tommi nodded, shooting a look at Zara, who was one of those people. She was huddled with a couple of other girls between the beds, gesturing dramatically with both hands as she talked.

"Are you doing hunters tomorrow?" Tommi asked, turning her attention back to Scott.

"Uh-huh, but mine's a large. I can sleep in." Scott turned his head as someone shouted his name. A second later a beer bottle came whizzing at his head. He lifted a hand just in time to catch it. "Thanks, dude!" he shouted to someone across the room.

Tommi couldn't help noticing the way his muscles flexed as he untwisted the cap. "Bummer for you," she said. "I'm doing the Larges, too. Hope you didn't have your heart set on another championship, because it's not going to happen."

"Oh yeah?" He took a swig, then grinned and wiped his mouth on the back of his hand. "Dream on. But hey, at least losing to me tomorrow will give you practice for losing to me again on Sunday."

"Guess again," Tommi retorted. "In case you haven't heard, my new eq horse is going to blow the socks off all the other nags here."

"In case *you* haven't heard, eq's judged on the rider, not the horse." Scott blinked. "But wait—*new* eq horse?" He sounded interested. "What do you mean?"

Tommi quickly filled him in on Orion's abscess. "But there's a serious silver lining," she finished. "Jamie just happened to have this awesome sale horse in the barn who's destined to be the next star. He's letting me lease him while Orion's out of commission."

"Interesting." Scott took a sip of his beer, not looking too impressed. "Well, if catch-riding your finals horse is what floats your boat . . ."

"Oh, it's no catch-ride—we're an amazing team." Tommi figured that wasn't really a lie. They *would* be a team by the time the competition rolled around. "But speaking of catch-riding, you'd better hope the judge doesn't ask us to switch horses as part of the test, because Fable's definitely not an easy ride." Tommi smirked. "I just make him look that way."

Scott grinned. "Don't worry. I'm used to a tough ride," he said. "If you end up having to ride my horse, you'll be crying for your mommy after the first fence."

"If you say so." Tommi raised her bottle. "May the best rider win."

Scott clinked his beer against hers. "Isn't that the point of the whole exercise?"

Tommi laughed. This party seemed a lot more fun than it had a few minutes ago. She could get used to having someone like Scott around—someone who wasn't afraid to dish it out *and* take it. It didn't hurt that he was super hot, smart, and a talented rider.

Too bad he lived so far away. Of course, Tommi had less than a year of high school left, and after that she could live anywhere she wanted. Maybe she should start looking at some West Coast colleges . . .

She grimaced, cutting off the thought before it could go any further. Scott noticed and leaned closer.

"You okay?" he said, actually looking a little worried. "I didn't freak you out with my awesomeness, did I?"

"Nope." Forcing all thoughts of the future out of her mind, Tommi smiled at him. "I was just hoping you're not going to embarrass yourself by crying after Fable plants you in the dirt on Sunday."

"Later," Zara said to the girl with the big nose whose name she'd already forgotten. "I want to grab another drink."

She hurried away, though she didn't bother heading for the beer in the bathroom or the sodas in the closet. Drinking wasn't her goal tonight.

Glancing around for her next victim, she was just in time to see that Scott guy drag Tommi over toward the dance bed. Laughing, Tommi kicked off her shoes and then climbed up there and started boogying. Scott jumped up and joined her.

Zara smiled. Tommi could be pretty uptight sometimes; it was nice to see her cutting loose. For a second she was tempted to go over and dance with them. Then the song switched to a lame old slow jam, and Scott caught Tommi by the wrist and pulled her close. Her arms slipped up over his shoulders, and their bodies pressed together as they swayed to the beat.

Okay, maybe not the best time to go over there. Besides, Zara really didn't have time to waste on dancing right now. This party wasn't about having fun—she was on a mission.

After another quick glance around, she made a beeline over to a tall, skinny girl with frizzy hair. "Hey," Zara greeted her. "Paris. How's it going?"

Paris blinked, looking confused for a second. No wonder. Zara had barely said two words to the girl before tonight, though they'd ridden in most of the same jumper classes all summer.

"Hey, Zara," Paris said, recovering quickly. "What's up? Cool party, huh?"

"Yeah, awesome." Zara glanced around, then leaned closer to the other girl. "Hey, listen, did you hear about the fight at my barn?"

Paris's eyes widened. "No!" she breathed. "What fight?"

"It went down like this. . . ." Zara quickly concocted a ridiculous story about Dani punching out one of the grooms because he'd forgotten to pack her bridle. It was hard to keep a straight face, but she managed.

By the end, Paris's eyes were practically bugging out of her head. "Whoa!" she said. "That's crazy! I never thought Dani was like that."

Oops. Too late, Zara remembered that Dani had ridden in most of those jumper classes, too. Plus she was so freakishly friendly that she knew just about everyone on the circuit. Probably better not to use her in the stories from now on.

"Well, that's just what I heard," Zara hedged, backing away. "It might not be true. Listen, I've got to . . ."

Without finishing, she edged behind a group of wide-eyed younger juniors and hurried into the bathroom. Two guys were in there digging through the beers in the bathtub.

"Hey, babe." The taller one looked Zara up and down. He was cute, lean and angular with cool amber eyes. "What's up? Want a drink?"

"Sure." Zara drained the rest of the beer she was holding and tossed it in the sink with the other empties. "Hit me."

The guy scooped a bottle out of the rapidly melting ice in the tub. With a flourish, he uncapped it and handed it over. "So I'm Chance," he said. "You're Zara Trask, right?"

"Yeah." The guy was definitely checking her out, big time, but Zara couldn't muster up any enthusiasm for flirting back. "Thanks for the beer, dude. See you."

She hurried out of the bathroom before the guy could respond. Leaning up against the wall, she took a sip and surveyed the room. She'd already spoken to several of the biggest gossips in the group, including Paris. Okay, so that story about Dani might've been a bust, but Zara was pretty sure that girl from Adam Dane's barn had totally believed her story about how one of the ponies from Pelham Lane had once belonged to the British royal family. Before that, Zara had gone up to a girl Marissa claimed was the biggest gossip in the entire state of Connecticut and pretended to be just drunk enough to "confess" to her that she was planning to audition for a certain popular TV singing competition. She'd come up with different wild tales for a couple of other well-known gossips at the party. If any of them were behind that blog, one of those stories was sure to be splashed all over it by tomorrow morning.

Zara rubbed her hands together, trying to figure out who else looked shady enough to be responsible. This was actually kind of fun, like being a secret agent or something. And the best part? She was sure her plan would help put a stop to HorseShowSecrets once and for all.

See? she thought, holding back a grin. *I always knew I could use my powers for good instead of evil!*

🐎

Kate glanced around the crowded hotel room, wondering what was taking Fitz so long. He'd left to grab them fresh drinks at least ten minutes ago, leaving her with Dani and a couple of her friends from different barns. Kate only knew the other girls slightly, and they were pretty much ignoring her as they chattered excitedly with Dani.

How did Dani do that, anyway? Kate watched as her barnmate threw back her head and laughed at something the others had said. Dani's family had more money than Kate's did, but not by that much—especially compared to most of the other people at this party. Her horse had been a bargain-priced Thoroughbred off the track, and both her saddle and her show boots had come from the local consignment shop. So how was it that Dani always seemed perfectly comfortable socializing in this world of imported warmbloods and custom everything? She had tons of friends at barns up and down the East Coast, while Kate always felt much more at home with the grooms than the clients.

One of the other girls, a short brunette, shrieked with laughter and smacked Dani on the arm, making her armful of silver bracelets jingle. Kate stared at the bracelets, wondering if they were real silver and how much they'd cost. Probably more than her entire wardrobe. Most of the time Kate didn't think much about stuff like that. What was the point? She had her life, and the rich girls had theirs. Being friends with Tommi and Zara had shown her that being wealthy didn't necessarily make everything easy.

Still, Kate couldn't help thinking sometimes that it had to make certain things a *little* easier.

"Sorry I took so long," Fitz's voice broke into her thoughts. "Got stuck talking to Chance—you know that guy never shuts up."

"It's okay." Kate wasn't sure who Chance was, but it didn't matter. She accepted the soda Fitz handed her, taking a sip.

"Hey," Dani said with a grin, nodding at the bottle in Fitz's hand. "Didn't you bring us all more beers? Rude!"

Fitz grinned. "Sorry, babe," he told Dani. "You've got two good legs now, right? I figured you'd want to use them."

The other two girls had turned to stare at Kate and Fitz, and they both laughed. "Burn," the short girl said, nudging Dani.

Meanwhile the other girl, a pretty blonde, was staring at Kate as if she was noticing her standing there for the first time. Which she probably was.

"Hey," the girl said, her gray eyes curious. "You're the one from the blog, right?" She glanced at Dani. "The girl who's supposed to take over your barn or whatever?"

"Duh, you know Kate." Dani drained the rest of her beer. "But listen, I really do need another. Anyone else?"

"Me!" the short brunette squealed. "I'll come with you."

"I'm good," the blonde said, still gazing at Kate.

As Dani and the brunette wandered off, another girl came racing over. "Fitz! Oh my god!" she cried, grabbing Fitz's arm and almost spilling his beer. "There you are—is that her?"

She stared at Kate. Kate stared back, feeling uneasy. She recognized this girl—her name was Gia, and she rode at

Kara Parodi's barn. Kate was pretty sure she was one of the many girls Fitz had hooked up with before he and Kate got together.

"Back off, G." Fitz put a protective arm around Kate. "It's just a rumor. For now, anyway."

Kate wished she could disappear. Had *everyone* seen that blog? Well, probably not—as far as she knew, Jamie and the rest of the adults still had no clue it existed. But thanks to that post about the assistant trainer job, Kate had become a celebrity to every junior on the circuit. Or maybe more like a freak-show attraction. Suddenly Kate had an inkling of how Zara must feel every day of her life.

"Okay, okay." Gia was still staring at Kate. "But listen, are you the same working student who's supposed to ride Charity's horse?"

"Huh?" Fitz looked confused. "What about Charity's horse?"

"Oh." Kate realized she'd never told him about that. "Um, yeah. Kara Parodi wants me to catch-ride something in the Large Juniors tomorrow. You know, if I can fit it in."

"Whoa!" Fitz grinned and kissed her. "That's awesome, babe! I can't believe you didn't tell me."

"Well, I haven't actually decided if I'm going to be able to do it yet." Kate was feeling more uncomfortable by the second.

Gia glanced around the room. "Yo, Charity!" she shouted, her voice surprisingly loud. "Over here!"

A moment later a petite dark-haired girl with a heart-shaped face and too much eyeliner hurried over. "What?" she demanded, frowning at Gia. "I was in the middle of something."

Gia waved toward Kate. "I found the girl Kara wants to ride Porter."

"Really?" Charity turned to study Kate. "Oh right, I've seen you," she said. "You ride that big gray in the eq, right?"

"Um, yeah." Kate leaned closer to Fitz. "I'm Kate."

"So how experienced are you?" Charity asked. "Because Porter can be strong and kind of a brat sometimes. He's super fancy though, and I don't want him to have a bad experience and, like, get ruined."

"Kate couldn't ruin a horse if she tried." Fitz was still smiling, though there was an edge to his voice. "Don't worry, she can ride your horse. Otherwise your trainer wouldn't have asked her, right?"

"Wait, are you guys talking about that horse Port Royal?" Kate had almost forgotten about Dani's blond friend until she spoke up. "Isn't he the one who dumped you at that show last month, Charity?"

"Oh. Hi, Reenie. I didn't notice you there." Charity frowned at the other girl. "Yeah, like I said, Porter's definitely *not* easy." Her gaze shifted back to Kate. "So do you do hunters much, or mostly just eq? Because Porter's definitely all hunter. He hates if you sit down on him too much, and—"

"Dude," Fitz broke in. "She'll be fine, okay? Chill."

"Easy for you to say, Fitz," Charity snapped. "It's not *your* fancy hunter we're talking about here."

"True." Fitz shrugged. "But as a matter of fact, Kate *is* training one of my fancy hunters, okay? You'll see him at the shows in Fl—uh, next spring, and he's going to kick all your horses' asses."

"Uh-oh, fighting words!" Gia put in with a grin.

Kate huddled even closer to Fitz. This time he seemed to notice her discomfort. "But enough about that," he told the other girls. "If you'll excuse us, we're going to go make out now."

Grabbing Kate's arm, he pulled her toward the door. "Thanks," she said as they emerged into the hallway. "That was . . . intense."

"Ignore those girls." Fitz wrapped his arms around Kate. He smiled as his face dipped toward hers. "Now, did someone mention something about making out?"

TWELVE

Tommi yawned as she yanked Fable's girth up another hole. The big gray gelding danced in place, almost stepping on her foot.

"Quit," Tommi mumbled. But she didn't have the energy to discipline him. Instead, she stepped back and let him finish his protest while she reached for her helmet.

She'd stayed way later at that party last night than she'd intended, and she was already regretting it. It was probably lucky that someone had finally complained to the front desk about all the noise and got things shut down a few minutes before midnight. Otherwise, who knew how long Tommi might have stayed. She'd been so busy lately with serious stuff—starting senior year, dealing with her father and her business plan, prepping for Indoors. She'd needed a chance to cut loose and have fun, and Scott Papadakis had helped her do just that. The two of them had danced, talked, had a few beers. And later, after the party broke up, they'd shared a little kiss-and-grope session in the hallway outside Tommi's room. She'd been tempted to invite him in, but luckily she'd resisted the urge.

"Okay, buddy." She clicked her helmet buckle shut, double-checked Fable's girth one more time, and gave him a pat on the neck. "Let's do this."

Soon she was riding into the big, rectangular indoor arena being used as a warm-up ring. A couple of trainers were school-ing in there already, but the crowds hadn't arrived yet to start warming up for the Small Junior Hunters, so Tommi was able to really get down to work. She'd gotten a taste of what Fable could do yesterday, but now she wanted to start getting to know him better.

She sent him into a trot, keeping Kate's tips in mind. Fable was fresh to start, and at first he resisted bending prop-erly around the turns, preferring to pop his shoulder and stare around at the handful of people watching from the stands on either side of the ring. But Tommi kept asking, and before long he started responding to her aids. For such a large horse, Fable was surprisingly agile, and by the time she brought him down for a walk break she was smiling. Okay, so she was still disap-pointed that Orion was out of commission for this show. But Fable wasn't a bad substitute. Not bad at all.

"Good boy." Tommi loosened the reins and leaned forward to give the horse a pat. As she straightened up again, she noticed a couple of people standing on the rail, waving in her direction. Tommi recognized Zara right away, but it took her a second to realize that was Scott standing beside her. Immediately, her heart jumped, and she wondered if she'd remembered to apply mascara that morning.

Then she shook her head, banishing such girlie thoughts.

Scott had seen her dressed to party last night, and now he was seeing her dressed to ride. That was life, and she was pretty sure he could handle it.

"Come on," she told Fable. "Let's go say hi."

She rode over to Zara and Scott. The arena was lower than the floor of the stands, so they were all at approximately the same eye level.

"Morning, sunshine," Zara greeted her. "Look who I found wandering around."

"Hey, Tommi." Scott looked none the worse for wear after their night of partying. "Can't believe you're riding already. I figured you'd be sound asleep until it's time for the Older Larges later."

"Sleep's a waste of time." Tommi patted Fable. "Couldn't resist coming by to check out the competition, huh?"

"Something like that." Scott grinned, then glanced at Zara. "Luckily I ran into your friend, and she told me you'd be here."

Tommi blinked at Zara. "Wait, shouldn't you be getting Ellie ready? You guys are doing the Older Smalls this morning, right?"

"Yeah, but Jamie just told me we're late in the order of go," Zara said. "He's going to text me when the guys have her ready to start warming up." She grimaced. "Wish I'd known the schedule before I dragged myself out of bed at the crack of dawn."

Scott was leaning on the rail, rubbing Fable's nose. The friendly gelding was snuffling at him, clearly hoping that a carrot or other treat might appear.

"So this is the future eq superstar, huh?" Scott said. "Looks pretty nice."

"He is. Like I said, he's going to help me kick your butt on Sunday." Tommi shot him a challenging look. "He did some dressage before he got imported and became a hunter, so his flatwork's amazing. Check it out." She sent Fable into a trot, lengthening and shortening his stride and then throwing in a few lateral movements for good measure. Hey, why not show off a little? It couldn't hurt to intimidate the competition before the class started.

When she rode back over to the rail, Zara was grinning and Scott actually looked kind of impressed. "Okay," he said. "But can he jump?"

"What do you think? Watch and learn." Tommi rode off again, this time aiming Fable at one of the warm-up fences. For the next few minutes she schooled him over all the jumps available. Fable was in a cooperative mood and seemed happy to do whatever Tommi asked, though he threw in a small buck when she flubbed the distance to the oxer, forcing him to land awkwardly. Tommi quickly got his attention back and spun him around in a dramatic rollback turn, galloping back to the oxer and clearing it perfectly this time.

There. That should impress Scott, she told herself as she brought the horse to a prompt, square halt.

She glanced over and saw Scott shooting her a thumbs-up. When she rode over, a little out of breath, he was grinning.

"Nice," he said. "Looks like he is the real deal—lucky you. Did you say he's one of Jamie's sale horses?"

"Uh-huh." Tommi rubbed Fable's neck, giving him a loose rein so he could reach for the treat Zara had just dug out of her pocket. "He's had him in the barn for maybe six or eight months, I think."

"Lucky you," Scott said again. Then he checked his watch. "Listen, I've got to go. Maybe I'll text you later?"

"You know where to find me." Tommi tried not to sound too eager. No sense letting him think she was all that interested. Even if she was.

"Cool. Later, ladies." He loped off toward the door.

"You two are so cute it's sickening." Zara glanced after Scott, then smirked at Tommi. "See? I told you it was love at first sight."

Tommi gathered up her reins. "Whatever," she said, though she couldn't help smiling. "I'd better finish before people start coming in to warm up for your division."

Zara hung out at the rail and watched Tommi finish her ride. Every few minutes, she pulled out her phone and refreshed the blog. Nothing had been posted since the previous afternoon, and she was getting impatient. Hadn't her brilliant plan worked?

She was staring at the phone, chewing her lower lip in frustration, when she realized Tommi was riding toward the exit. "Hold up!" Zara called, jogging along the rail. "I'll come with you."

Tommi dismounted and waited while Zara made her way down from the stands. Then they walked together through the tunnellike hallways leading back to the stabling area. When they arrived, Tommi slipped off Fable's bridle and clipped him into the cross-ties in the grooming stall.

"I'll help you untack if you want," Zara offered, slipping her phone into her pocket. "Got nothing better to do until it's my turn to ride."

"Cool, thanks." Tommi reached for the girth. "Can you get his boots?"

Zara bent to remove the gelding's open fronts. She straightened up just in time to see Kate coming toward them.

"Hey," Kate said. "How'd Fable do?"

Zara tossed the boots into Tommi's grooming bucket. "They looked amazing out there, especially for this ridiculously early in the morning," she told Kate.

"Yeah, he was great." Tommi pulled off her saddle. "He's really a whole different horse than the one I rode last spring—way more ridable and easier to get to focus. You've done an amazing job with him, Kate."

"Thanks." Kate grabbed a brush and started working the saddle marks out of Fable's coat. "I'm glad it worked out so you could ride him."

Tommi nodded, then shot Kate a sidelong glance. "Speaking of riding," she said. "What did you tell Kara Parodi about riding that hunter?"

Zara had almost forgotten about that. "You'd better say you're doing it," she told Kate. "For one thing, I definitely want to be there when you pin higher than Fitz."

Kate smiled weakly. "Actually, um, I haven't talked to Kara yet."

"You haven't?" Tommi sounded surprised, and maybe a smidge disapproving. "But the division starts later today."

"I know." Kate bent to run her brush over Fable's side, hiding her face from Zara and Tommi's view. "But I haven't run into her since we got here, and with things being so busy . . ."

"Well, you'd better track her down soon. She'll need to know if she's got to scratch the horse," Tommi said.

Zara rolled her eyes at the disapproving, almost teacherly tone of Tommi's voice. "She won't need to scratch, 'cause Kate's riding, right?" Zara poked Kate in the shoulder, making her jump and almost drop the brush she was holding.

"Um, I haven't actually decided yet," Kate said. "I mean, if there's any chance that rumor about Joy's job is true . . ."

Tommi shook her head. "Come on, Kate. That rumor is totally bogus, and you know it."

"We don't know that," Zara put in. She'd been so busy with her sleuthing that she'd almost forgotten about that particular rumor for a while. But now she glanced curiously at Kate. "So does this mean you're thinking about taking the job?"

"Of course she's not," Tommi said before Kate could answer. "Kate's not stupid enough to even consider accepting a job like that at her age."

Kate kept her gaze on Fable as she responded, though Zara could see that she was frowning. Her voice was quiet when she spoke. "It's not like I *asked* for the job or anything."

"Not the point." Tommi grabbed a brush and ran it down Fable's legs. "Like I've said a million times, I'm sure it's not even true. Jamie knows better than to ask you to drop out of school and risk, like, your whole future on something like that."

Kate shot her a look. "In case you've forgotten, it's not like I can afford to do this any other way," she snapped.

Tommi blinked and straightened up. "Huh? Do what? What are you talking about?"

"This!" Kate waved a hand at the stabling area. "Riding, showing, all of it. The only way I get to do it is by working for it. Getting an A on my chemistry test isn't going to win me any rides on a nice hunter."

Zara winced at the raw ache in Kate's voice. "It's cool," she put in quickly. "We all know how hard you work, Kate. That's why it's easy to believe Jamie would want you to take over Joy's job."

"You're not helping." Tommi scowled at her, then returned her attention to Kate. "Look, you might think you can't afford to turn this job down. But the best way to guarantee you'll be able to keep doing what you love is to stay in school, go to college, all that jazz. Then you'll have choices."

"Thanks, Dad," Kate muttered.

Yikes. Zara wasn't used to seeing either of her friends this worked up—especially at each other. "Chill, you guys," she said. "It'll work out, okay? It's not like half of the stuff on that blog is true anyway."

"Yeah, you're right. I'm sure it's not true." Tommi kept her gaze on Kate. "But just in case it is—"

"I'll deal with it, okay?" Kate's jaw was clenched. "I don't need you to tell me what to do."

"I'm just trying to help!" Tommi sounded slightly annoyed now. "I mean, everybody else around here is acting like, oh goody, Kate's going to be the assistant trainer, whoop-di-do! It's just not realistic—somebody has to be the one to tell you that."

"Okay, I think she gets it." Zara felt kind of weird playing peacemaker. It wasn't exactly her usual role. But Tommi was coming on pretty strong, and Zara could tell that Kate wasn't dealing with it too well. No wonder. After what she'd confided in Zara about her parents and her grades, she was clearly a bit on edge. Having Professor Tommi lecture her about staying in school? Probably not what she needed right then. Not that it was *ever* much fun to have someone telling you what to do when you didn't want to do it. Zara knew that from experience.

Just then they all heard laughter from around the corner. A second later Marissa and Dani wandered into view.

"Hey!" Marissa exclaimed when she saw Zara and the others. "We were just talking about you guys."

Dani grinned. "Well, *one* of you, anyway. Specifically, the one who was seen getting awfully friendly with a certain adorable West Coast eq star last night?" She waggled her eyebrows in Tommi's direction.

"Tell us everything, Tommi," Marissa said with a giggle. "We want to get the scoop before it turns up on the blog later."

The blog. Suddenly Zara realized she hadn't checked it in like fifteen minutes. Pulling out her phone, she hit refresh. This time the latest headline read PARTY TIME AT HARRISBURG!

Zara grinned. Her plan had worked! Now to see which of her planted stories had done the trick.

As she scanned the rest of the post, her heart fell. None of the stories were there. Just a fairly generic post about the party, describing some of the action and going on to mention that hotel management had broken it up and a few of the attendees had gotten in trouble with their trainers.

Zara frowned. Her plan should have worked. Had she missed someone? Or had the blogger caught on that her story was fake? Either way, it looked like she was going to have to come up with something else.

Just then her phone buzzed in her hand. "Uh-oh, there's Jamie," she said, scanning the text. "I've got to go."

"Good luck!" Dani said. "We'll be cheering you and Ellie on."

"Thanks, guys." Zara switched off her phone and stuck it in her pocket, trying to remember where she'd left her jacket and helmet as she headed down the aisle to find Jamie.

"That's good." Jamie waved Zara over as she circled back after a warm-up jump. "We don't want to overdo it—she's ready."

"Yeah, she's feeling good." Zara grinned and patted her mare, who was feeling a little more amped than ideal for a hunter. But it was too late to work her down now; Zara would just have to hope that Ellie put the extra energy into a back-cracking jump instead of, say, bucking off her rider in the corner. Either way, it was sure to be a fun trip.

She walked the horse beside Jamie as they headed over to the show ring. Ellie's ears swiveled in every direction as they reached the underground hallway leading into the big main arena. Several other horses were there waiting for their turns, with nervous-looking riders listening to last-minute advice from their trainers. On either side, a wide concourse curved away around the base of the massive bleachers overhead. Rows of vendors selling tack, gifts, and other stuff were set up there, and people were wandering and shopping.

Zara halted Ellie behind a sweet-faced dapple gray that looked like an oversize pony. Halt wasn't Ellie's favorite gait, and she jigged in place, twisting her head and clanking her teeth against the bit. Jamie reached up to rub the mare's neck.

"Just keep her quiet," he told Zara. "And don't forget to let her take a peek at that jump with the yellow flowers on your opening circle."

"I know, you told me that like three times already. I'm on

it." Zara felt a nervous little shiver go through her as she watched the girl on the dapple gray ride forward to take her turn in the ring. Ellie picked up on her nerves, suddenly spooking away from a man coming out of the tack vendor's stall on the right with a rustling plastic bag.

"Easy, girl," Jamie murmured.

Zara knew she had to take her mind off the coming round. Ellie was so ridiculously sensitive she could practically read her rider's mind. Well, the bad parts, anyway. She certainly never seemed to be able to tell when Zara was thinking it was way past time for a lead change.

Feeling a nervous giggle coming on, Zara cleared her throat and glanced down at Jamie. Suddenly she thought of the perfect distraction.

"Hey," she said. "I heard Joy's pregnant. True?"

Okay, that worked. Zara forgot all about everything else as she watched Jamie's jaw twitch in shock. He glanced up at her, his blue eyes troubled.

"Where—uh, where did you hear that?" he asked. "I didn't think Joy had told anyone else yet."

Zara's eyes widened. "So it's true? Oh my god!"

"You didn't hear it from me," Jamie said hurriedly. "And listen, Zara, it's really not something you kids should be gossiping about, okay? Joy will make an announcement when she's ready, and until then I hope you'll all respect her privacy."

"Sure, of course." Zara didn't bother to tell him that ship had sailed. Her mind raced, trying to figure out what this meant. If the rumor about Joy's pregnancy was true, was the part about Kate and the job true, too? She sneaked a peek at Jamie, trying to decide if she should just come right out and ask him. She'd probably be doing Kate a favor; not knowing was obviously stressing her out . . .

"Zara." Jamie patted her on the leg, his voice and expression suddenly all business again. "You're up."

"Huh?" Zara blinked. Oh right. She gathered up her reins, kicking Ellie forward. "Okay, girlie. Here goes nothing."

THIRTEEN

Kate was wiping down one of Jamie's saddles when she realized she'd lost track of time. Uh-oh. Had she missed Zara's first hunter round? She'd been planning to take a break and go watch. She always liked to cheer for her friends' rides when she could, and Zara had been so nice to her about the whole school thing yesterday that Kate felt a special desire to support her.

She checked her watch and winced. Unless things were running *really* late, Zara had probably finished already. Still, she couldn't resist checking. After tossing the saddle back on the rack, she jogged over to the ring. There was no sign of Zara or Jamie or anyone else from Pelham Lane. She did spy another familiar face, though.

"Kate!" Kara Parodi strode toward her, a slight frown on her face. "I was just about to come track you down." She shot a look over her shoulder at an anxious-looking junior on a stout bay gelding. "I don't have much time, but I need to know if you can ride that horse for me later."

Kate froze, feeling trapped and helpless. The truth was, she still wasn't sure how to respond. Part of her longed to say yes. This was exactly the kind of scenario she'd dreamed about all those years ago when she was riding scruffy ponies with Nat at Happy Acres. Back then the closest she got to the A circuit was pretty pictures in glossy magazines.

But this wasn't just about her, was it? Kate was at this show to work for Jamie, not to flit around fulfilling all her childhood dreams. And if there was any chance that job rumor might be true, she couldn't risk her entire future for one ride, no matter how amazing it was. Couldn't chance having Jamie change his mind about her. Couldn't stand seeing that much more important and practical opportunity slip away.

"I—I meant to tell you sooner," she blurted out, twisting her hands together so hard her knuckles cracked. "Something came up, and I can't do it. I'm sorry."

Kara frowned. "Are you sure? Because when I didn't hear back from you, I sort of assumed you were in."

"I'm sorry." Kate couldn't think of anything else to say, and if she tried too hard she was afraid she might start crying. "I'm really sorry. Thanks, um, thanks for the offer, though."

The other trainer didn't respond, though her eyes flashed with irritation. "Kara!" the bay horse's rider called out, sounding panicky. "Can you come here? I think my girth is loose."

"Coming." Kara spun on her heel and marched over to her rider without another glance at Kate. Kate slipped away into the crowd, feeling about as worthwhile as a clump of manure on someone's shoe.

"Nice rounds, Zara." Some random girl smiled as Zara hurried past. "Love your horse!"

"Thanks." Zara didn't slow down. She wasn't in the mood for small talk with strangers. Now that she was finished riding for the day, she had work to do.

She ditched her jacket and helmet in the tack stall, grabbing the hoodie she'd left there earlier. In the pocket were a notepad and pen she'd swiped from the hotel lobby that morning. Since last night's plan hadn't worked, she'd decided it was time to approach the problem from a different angle. Zara slipped on the hoodie, yanking at the top few buttons of her show shirt. It was no wonder they called the collar at the top a choker.

Now all she had to do was find a private spot where she could focus for a while. If she tried to find a spot in the stands overlooking the ring, someone was sure to spot her and come over wanting to chat. Even the warm-up ring probably wasn't safe.

Heading past the tiny extra schooling ring into the tunnel, she turned down one of the curved hallways of the concourse. She paused and glanced at the tack vendor on the end, tempted to go in and browse. She could use some new paddock boots.

But no. Resisting the temptation, she hurried past, ignoring the other booths as well. She could shop *after* she exposed the blogger.

She kept walking until she hit a spot where there were no vendors nearby, just a bunch of extra trash cans and a stack of folding chairs on a rolling cart. She grabbed one of the chairs, unfolding it and setting it up between the cart and the wall.

She sat down, feeling pleased with herself—almost like a real detective or spy or something. There. Now the people wandering past wouldn't even be able to see her.

Then she took out her notebook, pen, and smartphone. Pulling up the blog, she started scrolling through the posts again. This time, she jotted down the basics of each story—who, what, when, where, why, how. Those were the questions you needed to answer to solve a mystery. Zara had learned that during several boring weeks she'd spent on the set of one of her mother's movies one summer. It had been a crime caper, and the guy playing the main detective had loved spouting off about all the Method research he'd done to get ready for the part. Who knew something like that would come in handy someday?

Zara quickly filled several pages with notes. First she needed to figure out how many of the stories on the blog were actually true. Anybody could have made up the stuff that wasn't true, like the rumor about Zac. But once she'd confirmed the real stories, she could start interviewing people, trying to figure out who had been around at the time the events in question were happening. Like, who had witnessed each event, and how many people they had told. Stuff like that. By cross-referencing that information with what she was writing down now, Zara hoped she'd be able to narrow down her list of suspects and eventually unmask the blogger.

She was so focused on what she was doing that the sound of someone clearing his throat made her jump and almost fall off her chair. Looking up, she saw a guy lounging with one elbow propped on the stack of chairs, watching her.

Not just *any* guy, either. He definitely wasn't a rider—Zara would have known that at first glance, even if he wasn't wearing a uniform indicating he was part of the janitorial staff. He was probably in his early or mid-twenties, lean but muscular, with floppy black hair falling over his eyes and some serious stubble.

"Hey, babe," he said. "Nice hideout. You got room for one more back there?" His gaze slipped to the cleavage peeking out at the top of her unbuttoned show shirt, leaving no doubt as to his intentions.

She smiled automatically. Skeevy but hot? Just her type.

At the same time, she felt a flash of annoyance. Why did he have to interrupt her just when she was making progress?

"Get lost," she said. "I'm busy, and I'm pretty sure you're supposed to be working, not hitting on underage girls."

The guy's mouth twisted, and he backed up a step. "Okay, chill out," he said. "I was just being friendly, all right?"

"Great. Go be friendly to someone else. I'm busy."

"Freaking horse show snobs," the guy muttered.

Zara felt a twinge of regret as he grabbed one of the spare trash cans and disappeared. Too bad. He could've been fun. Somehow, though, she couldn't get too worked up about it. She just wasn't in the mood for that kind of thing right now. Whatever.

Returning her attention to her phone, she got back to work. Just a few more posts to go through, and she'd be ready to start interviewing people.

"Kate. Can I talk to you for a minute?"

Kate jumped and spun around. She'd been so focused on sweeping up some spilled shavings in the aisle that she hadn't heard Jamie coming. "Um, sure." She couldn't help noticing the troubled look on the trainer's face. "What is it?"

Jamie glanced at Marissa, who was fussing over her horse as Elliot tacked it up nearby. None of the other older juniors were tacking up for the Large Junior Hunters yet, but Marissa always liked to be in the saddle well before the division started. Her gelding, Miles, an experienced show horse with a placid temperament, didn't need the extra time, but Marissa did. She always told Kate it settled her nerves to walk around for a while before beginning her real warm-up.

Jamie took Kate by the elbow and steered her around the corner into an empty stall. Kate clutched her broom in her other hand, wondering what was going on. An empty stall was about as close to a private spot as there was in the cramped indoor stable area. That meant whatever Jamie wanted to talk to her about had to be serious.

"I just ran into Kara Parodi," Jamie said. "She told me she asked you to catch-ride something for her today, and you said no."

Panic shot through Kate. Would Jamie hold it against her for even being *asked* to ride for another trainer? Was that why his expression was so solemn? Her mind raced, trying to come up with something to say.

"Um . . . ," she began.

"Look." Jamie ran a hand over his face, suddenly looking way too tired for late morning. "Kara's a good person and an excellent horsewoman, but she's not the forgiving type when she thinks someone screwed her over. I need to know why you left her hanging till the last minute—and why you said no."

"I—I—" Kate swallowed hard. Jamie didn't seem angry,

just confused. "I didn't think you'd want me to ride for another barn."

Jamie sighed. "That's what I was afraid of. Look, Kate, lots of juniors catch-ride for other barns all the time—you know that. It's no big deal."

"I know, but . . ." Kate's voice trailed off. She didn't dare mention that job rumor, though it filled her mind. Didn't that change things?

"I appreciate your loyalty." The corners of Jamie's mouth turned up in a wry half smile. "But it's not necessary in this case, I promise. If you weren't sure what to do, I wish you'd come to me to talk about it. I would have told you to go for it."

"Really?"

"Definitely. You're the hardest worker I know, Kate—I want you to have exactly these kinds of opportunities. I'm just sorry I didn't have anything to offer you this time myself."

"Oh. Thanks." Kate tried to return his smile, but it wasn't easy. She'd really blown it this time. Kara Parodi had offered her the chance of a lifetime, and Kate had turned it down. And for what? Nothing, apparently.

Jamie was still smiling. "I hope you brought some better breeches than that," he said, gesturing to Kate's well-worn schooling tights. "Because Kara likes her riders turned out to the nines."

"Huh?" Kate shook her head, wondering if Jamie had missed the point of this whole conversation. "But I—I said no."

"I know. Lucky for you, *I* said yes." Jamie cocked an eyebrow. "I even managed to make Kara think the misunderstanding was all my fault, so she wouldn't think you were jerking her around."

Kate just stared at him for a moment, not sure she was hearing him right. "You said yes?" she echoed numbly. "You mean I'm showing that horse?"

"Yeah, if you're interested. I can still call Kara and take it back, but I hope I don't have to. For one thing, she might never speak to me again." He smiled to show that he was kidding—mostly—but his eyes were serious as he watched Kate carefully. "More importantly, I think it will be a great experience for you. So what do you say? You up for it?"

"Yes," Kate blurted out, so overwhelmed by what was happening that she could barely think straight. She'd always known that Jamie was the best in the business in every possible way. This just proved it. Who *wouldn't* want to work for a guy like that?

"Good." Jamie looked pleased. "I hear the horse is a tough ride, though, so get your game face on." He plucked the broom out of her hand. "I'll get someone else to finish up here—you'd better hurry and get changed. Your division starts in an hour."

FOURTEEN

"Good boy," Tommi murmured, giving Toccata a pat and smiling as she heard Zara whooping from the stands nearby. She'd just finished her first hunter round, and it had gone really well. Toccata was focused and jumping like a freak of nature, and Tommi had found every spot and made it look easy.

Jamie and Javier were waiting just outside the ring. The young groom immediately took hold of Toccata's bridle, murmuring soothing words to the horse as Tommi dismounted.

"Well done," Jamie said. "You two looked good out there."

"Thanks." Tommi gave Toccata a quick pat as Javier led him off toward the stalls. Then she unhooked her helmet. "He's really on his game today."

"Feeling ready for the handy?" Jamie asked.

"Yeah, we've got it. I've been working with him on trotting jumps all year, remember? He thinks they're boring now."

The handy hunter round, which was coming up as soon as everyone had finished the first round, was the reason Tommi and Toccata had ended up out of the ribbons at Harrisburg last year. They'd been eating up the course until they came to the trot jump, which Toccata had taken as an invitation to act silly and pretend he'd never been asked to do such a thing in his life. She'd barely gotten him over it on the third try—totally embarrassing, and not a moment she planned to repeat.

Jamie nodded, his gaze wandering to Marissa, who was up next. She was sitting on her horse halfway down the entryway, huddled over and looking as if she might be sick at any moment. "We'll talk later, okay?" Jamie told Tommi.

"Sure." Tommi didn't need Jamie to go over her round with her to know it had been pretty close to perfect.

She was smiling as she turned around, planning to head up to where Zara was sitting and watch Marissa and Fitz go. Kate wasn't riding until later—Tommi hoped she'd be able to watch her before she had to warm up for her handy round. She'd been thrilled when Fitz texted to say that Kate had accepted that catch-ride. Apparently Jamie had talked her into it or something. Tommi wasn't sure of the details, but she figured Zara might know. Ever since she'd started her campaign to identify that blogger, the girl had been on top of every bit of news and gossip out there.

As Tommi started up the steps into the stands, someone came barreling down toward her. "Sorry," Tommi said automatically, starting to step back out of the way.

"Don't be sorry." It was Scott. He grinned and took her by the arm, steering her up to the nearest landing. "That was an amazing round."

"Oh! Hi." Tommi's elbow felt warm where he'd touched it, even through layers of show shirt and jacket. "I heard yours was good, too. Didn't get to see you go—I was warming up."

"It's okay, I don't blame you for not wanting to watch and get psyched out." He laughed, then reached out and took her hand. "Seriously, though, you were amazing. Glad I got to see it."

"Thanks." Tommi's heart thumped as he squeezed her hand, and they just stood there smiling at each other. For a second she wondered if that blogger was watching. Would she and Scott end up a featured story tomorrow?

She shook off the thought. What did she care if they did? She and Scott were both young, single, and interested. Nothing wrong with that. Not that her love life was the world's business, but hey, she'd had worse things written about her.

"Hey, my friend's up next," she said, noticing that Marissa was performing her opening circle.

"Cool. Let's watch." He pulled her toward a row of seats, stepping back to let her go in first. Always the gentleman, huh? Nice.

Tommi leaned her elbows on her knees, watching as Marissa aimed her horse at the first fence. She looked tense, but Miles was used to ignoring that. The horse yanked up his knees, sailing over the fence like a pro.

"Easy, easy," Tommi murmured under her breath, her muscles automatically tensing into a half-halt as she saw Miles building speed toward the next jump.

"Ouch," Scott said as the pair ended up chipping in.

That error seemed to wake Miles up, though, and the horse adjusted his own stride on the approach to the next one. The rest of the round was decent, though Tommi knew there was no way it would make the cutoff. Still, she guessed that Marissa was probably just happy to survive without fainting or falling off or something. That wouldn't be good enough for Tommi, but not everyone was as competitive as she was.

Then again, some people were. She shot a look over at Scott.

"So are you ready for Sunday?" she asked him.

"Haven't really started thinking about eq yet." His quick sideways glance told Tommi that probably wasn't true, but she let it slide.

"Must be nice to be competing on a familiar horse," she said. "Still, that'll make it even sweeter when Fable and I beat your pants off."

"Already trying to get my pants off, huh?" Scott raised an eyebrow and smirked, glancing down at his breeches. "Can't wait."

Tommi blushed. "That's not what I meant, you perv." She smacked him on the arm, then leaned back and watched the next rider come into the ring. "Anyway, Fable and I aren't slacking off. We'll be in the ring Saturday night making sure we're ready. Jamie thinks if we get in there around eleven or so, it won't be crowded."

"Maybe not, but I can guarantee there will be at least one other horse in there." Scott shrugged. "I was planning to school around that time myself."

"Then I guess we'll see you there." Tommi knew she shouldn't be so excited about that. She and Fable really did need all the schooling they could get if she wanted to have a chance of pinning.

Still, maybe having Scott there would be a good thing. Tommi always performed best under pressure, right? Besides, having Scott around might distract her just enough to keep her show nerves at bay.

"Yeah." Scott sounded pleased, too. "Guess we will."

🐎

"How do I look?" Kate spun around slowly. "Any hay on my jacket? Hair sticking out?"

Fitz was lounging on one of the director's chairs in Pelham Lane's tack stall. Even though his handy round was still to come, he'd swapped out his tall boots for his favorite shabby old boat shoes, and his jacket, tie, and helmet were nowhere in sight. He stood, stretched, and stepped over to tweak Kate's helmet, straightening it.

"You look perfect." He cupped a hand around her neck, planting a whisper-soft kiss on the tip of her nose. "Gorgeous. Like always."

Kate reached back to make sure he hadn't messed up her hair, feeling rushed, nervous, and a little exasperated. This wasn't the time for Fitz to play Mr. Romance. Didn't he know that?

"Seriously, I'm not looking for compliments," she told him. "I don't want to look like a slob when I see Kara Parodi."

"Seriously." Fitz stepped back and smiled at her. "You look like a total pro. No horse slobber on your breeches, no toilet paper hanging off your boot, no boogers hanging out of your nose. Now let's go find your horse."

That made Kate laugh. "Okay, thanks." She stepped over for one last check in the mirror hanging on one canvas wall. She was dressed in the best show clothes she could manage. Her tall boots were old and off-the-rack, but she took good care of them and they fit her well. She'd found her jacket on the clearance rack of the local consignment shop, marked way down due to a small tear in a shoulder seam that had taken Nat all of five minutes to repair.

Kate felt a pang as her fingers slipped up toward the site of that rip. But no—she didn't have time to think about Nat right now. Instead, she turned her gaze to her Tailored Sportsman breeches, checking for any stray bits of hay or shavings. Those breeches were among the nicest things she owned; they'd been an early Christmas gift from Tommi, and sometimes Kate felt funny about wearing them anywhere near a horse. But they definitely helped her look the part now.

Fitz was watching her. "Enough primping, princess," he joked, grabbing her hand. "We'd better get you over there."

Kate knew he was right. She definitely didn't want to be late meeting Kara. She let Fitz pull her along the aisles and hallways of the show complex. When they reached the warm-up ring, Kate immediately spotted Kara standing by one of the jumps, schooling several riders.

"Wish me luck," Kate said with a shiver.

"You don't need it. You're going to do great." Fitz kissed her once more, then gave her a gentle shove into the ring. "Knock 'em dead, gorgeous."

Kate tossed him a quick smile, then hurried into the ring, pausing to let a rider canter past. It wasn't until the girl aimed her horse at Kara's jump that Kate realized it was Charity, the owner of the gelding she was supposed to ride. Her current mount was a heavily built old-style warmblood mare with a massive head. The horse heaved itself over the jump and cantered away.

"Great," Kara called. "Who's next?"

As the trainer glanced around, she spotted Kate. She waved her over, and Kate hurried to join her beside the jump.

"Good, you're here." Kara grabbed the phone off her belt and sent a quick text. "Liam will bring the horse in and help you get mounted. Go ahead and get warmed up, and let me know when you're ready to jump."

Kate glanced at the entrance. A groom had just appeared leading a tall bay horse with a long neck and a graceful jig. "Thanks. Um, any advice?"

"He likes support with the reins but not much leg. When I rode him this morning he was spooking at everything, so be ready." Kara spun around and jabbed a finger at one of her riders. "No, no, no, Merri!" she shouted. "I told you, you've got to *ride*, not just sit there!"

Deciding she'd been dismissed, Kate waited for a girl on a big gray to thunder past, then jogged over to the entrance. The groom was tugging lightly on the reins and humming as the bay horse snorted and eyed the action in the ring.

"Hi," Kate said. "Um, I'm Kate. The catch-rider?"

"So you're the one they picked to be Porter's next victim, eh?" The groom had a lopsided smile and an Irish accent. "Lucky you."

"He's not that bad, is he?" Kate stepped over to pat the horse, who snuffled at her curiously.

The groom chuckled. "Nah. Only to hear his owner tell it." He winked and shot a look at Charity, who was circling around to the jump again. "Need me to help swap out for your saddle?"

Kate smiled uncertainly. "Um, no thanks. That is, I don't

have a saddle. I mean . . ." She glanced helplessly at the saddle on the horse.

"No worries." The groom shrugged. "Guess that's why Kara wanted him tacked up like this. I was wondering, but it doesn't do to ask too many questions when she's in show mode, know what I mean?" He winked again, then turned to pull down the nearest stirrup. "Let's get these adjusted, then."

As soon as Kate mounted, most of her nerves fled. This was her thing, the place she felt most at home. The horse shifted his weight beneath her, giving her a hint of his hair-trigger athleticism.

"Good boy," she murmured, gathering up the reins. "Let's see if we're going to get along, all right?"

It felt like seconds later that Kate was staring out through the tunnel into the main ring. The warm-up had gone well. Porter wasn't an easy ride, but he wasn't as difficult as Kate had been expecting, either—sensitive, maybe a little insecure, but a real tryer. He'd overjumped the first warm-up fence by about a foot, eliciting snickers from a few of the watching riders, including Charity. Kate had stayed with him easily, though, pushing him forward and bringing him around again, steadying him more firmly on the second try. That time he'd sailed over in perfect hunter form, and Kara had actually smiled and shot Kate a thumbs-up.

Now the trainer was standing beside Porter, holding his bridle and barking out instructions that Kate barely heard. It was almost their turn to head into the ring. Was this really happening? Kate had ridden in her share of junior hunter classes at shows up and down the East Coast. But this was different. This was *Indoors*.

"Okay, you're up." Kara let go of the bridle and stepped back as the gate swung open. "Go!"

Kate took a deep breath, urging Porter forward into the show ring. He was alert, and she could feel his muscles bunching as he looked for something to spook at. She ignored that, pushing him forward into a brisk trot and then asking for a leg yield to give him something else to think about. Still, she couldn't blame him for being nervous. Her own stomach was fluttering like crazy, and her palms felt clammy beneath her gloves. Why did the arena look so much bigger now than it had when she'd been sitting out there earlier, watching other people ride?

Porter swerved, eyeing a large white banner hanging on the arena wall, and Kate realized she had to focus. "Come on, now," she whispered, half-halting softly. "Let's not be silly, okay?"

She slipped her outside heel back, sending the horse into a canter so smooth and silky Kate couldn't help smiling, just as she had when she'd first felt it back in the warm-up ring. No wonder Kara and the horse's owner had been so eager to get him into the show ring. If his rider could convince him to concentrate on his job, Porter could be a world-beater.

And for right now, it was Kate's job to make him look like exactly that. She sent him in a big, loopy circle around the jumps, letting him take a peek at several of the spookier ones. At the same time, she kept him softly but consistently on the aids, not letting him think for a second that he could get away with anything. It hadn't taken more than a few minutes in the warm-up to realize that was the way this horse needed to be ridden. A hunter round was supposed to look easy and effortless, but often a whole lot of effort was going on behind that pretty picture.

Kate felt light-headed as she turned the horse toward the first jump, a solid-looking vertical off a long approach. Was she really here, or was this a dream? She almost closed her eyes as she felt the horse's muscles bunch in front of the fence, but she resisted the urge. They sailed over, and Kate felt Porter's muscles bunch again as if he were thinking about tossing in a celebratory buck. Kate closed her leg, sending him forward to short-circuit that idea. The horse responded well, flowing smoothly toward the next obstacle.

By the time they finished the course, Kate was smiling. She could hear people cheering as she rode toward the gate. Glancing up at the stands, she picked out Tommi, Zara, and Fitz in the front row. All three of them were on their feet, whooping and waving wildly. She grinned at her friends but didn't dare wave back; Kara was waiting at the gate.

The trainer was smiling when Kate reached her. "That was terrific," she said. "Good job. Find Liam and tell him to cool him out and keep him calm until the handy." Then she turned away and crooked a finger at Charity, who was sitting a few feet away on her big mare. "You're up. Let's go."

Charity urged her horse forward, staring at Kate. Kate smiled uncertainly, waiting for Porter's owner to say something, to acknowledge what a truly nice horse she was lucky enough to own. But Charity didn't say a word, turning her gaze toward the ring and riding past.

Kate shrugged. Riding over to a clear spot in the passageway, she slid down and gave Porter a pat before running up the stirrups. "You were amazing, big guy," she whispered. "Thank you."

By the next afternoon, Kate was half convinced that this entire weekend had to be a dream. Porter's handy hunter round had been almost as spectacular as his first round, with only a slight bobble on the rollback to the third fence. Kara had warned her that the horse could be fussy and a little aggressive when he felt crowded, so in the under-saddle class Kate had worked hard to keep her mount away from the other horses as much as possible, and to distract him when someone did get too close. She'd been vaguely aware of Tommi, Fitz, Marissa, and Charity passing now and then, but had kept most of her attention on her own horse, using every trick she knew to keep him focused.

And it had worked—they'd placed second to Tommi and Toccata in the class. Still, even after two more great jumping rounds today, Kate had hardly dared to believe it when she heard they'd finished third and fourth that day. Tommi and Toccata were champions, and Kate finished just off reserve. She'd beaten Fitz and his hunter, Tommi's new friend Scott, Charity and Marissa. It was an amazing experience.

Kate was standing in the aisle near the Pelham Lane tack stall with several of the other juniors when she heard the news. "Congratulations!" Marissa exclaimed, grabbing Kate and jumping up and down. "You're amazing!"

Fitz was tall enough to lean right over Marissa's head and plant a kiss on Kate's lips. "That's our little superstar," he said. "I always knew you were destined for greatness."

"It's nice to meet a man who isn't threatened when his woman kicks his butt." Zara smirked at Fitz. "And she so totally did, by the way."

Marissa let go of Kate. "Where's Tommi? We should congratulate her, too."

"I think she's off handwalking Toccata somewhere." Dani pulled out her smartphone. "I'll text her and find out where she is."

Kate didn't hear what the others said after that. She'd just spotted Kara Parodi standing out in the open area in front of the rows of stalls, talking to another trainer. "Be right back," she told her friends.

She hurried over, waiting until Kara finished her conversation with the other trainer and then tapping her on the arm.

"Excuse me," Kate said. "I just wanted to thank you again. You know—for the opportunity. Porter's a great horse."

Kara looked pleased. "Yeah, I guess you just proved that to everyone," she said. "You did great, Kate. I'm glad this worked out."

Before Kate could respond, Charity stomped over to them. "Oh, it's you," she greeted Kate with a frown. "Thanks for making me look bad."

"Uh, what?" Kate blurted out.

"Charity, that's enough." Kara's voice was sharp. "We agreed that you didn't want to ride Porter at this show, and Kate was kind enough to step in. End of story." Her words held a strong hint of warning.

Charity glared at her, then at Kate. Finally she shrugged. "Whatever," she muttered. "I'm going back to the hotel."

She stormed off. Kara shook her head. "Sorry about that," she told Kate. "It's not you, it's her, if you know what I mean."

"It's okay." Kate smiled weakly, then wandered back over to rejoin her friends, who had drifted closer while she was talking to Kara.

"What was that all about?" Zara asked, glancing after Charity.

Kate swallowed hard. She hadn't realized her friends had witnessed the exchange with Porter's owner.

Dani smirked. "Isn't it obvious? Little Miss Snotface didn't like having Kate whip her butt on her own horse."

Fitz saw Kate's expression and threw an arm around her. "Don't let it bother you, babe," he said. "Dani's right—that girl's just being a sore loser."

"I guess." Kate tossed one last glance in the direction Charity had disappeared. "Anyway, it's no big deal." Doing her best to shake off the momentary dark spot in her perfect day, she smiled at the others. "Did you guys find Tommi? We should go congratulate her, like you said."

Kate was still in a daze as she picked out Fable's stall that evening. Most of the competitors had gone back to their hotels an hour ago, but Kate was in no hurry to leave. She wanted to savor this day as long as possible. Even if she never got to do it again; even if she spent the rest of her horse-show career scooping poop and warming up bratty ponies at midnight, it had been worth it for those few glorious moments in the big ring.

"Your turn starts soon, big guy," she murmured to the

burly gray horse, who was watching with interest as she sifted through the bedding in his stall. "You'd better be good for Tommi, you hear?"

In response, Fable stuck his nose in his water bucket and splashed half of it out onto himself and the floor. Kate sighed and smiled, shooing him away so she could remove the wet shavings. Fable was definitely a character. It still felt a little strange that Tommi was going to be the one to ride him in his first eq finals, but Kate was trying hard to remember that he wasn't her horse, even if he felt like it sometimes. Besides, it was only for a show or two. Soon Tommi's eq horse would be better, and Fable would go back to being Kate's project.

"And by this time next year, who knows?" she whispered with a shiver, remembering those amazing trips with Porter and imagining the even more incredible feeling of entering the ring with a horse she'd worked with all year long. A horse that felt *almost* like her own.

Kate had already picked out several other stalls, and her wheelbarrow was almost full, so she gave Fable one last scratch in his favorite itchy spot between his ears and then let herself out of his stall. After she dumped the wheelbarrow and returned it to its spot behind the stalls, she went back to refill Fable's bucket, warning him not to spill it this time. Then she wandered into the tack room, her eyes immediately drawn to the multicolored row of ribbons hanging on the wall. She hadn't gotten to keep the ones she and Porter won—his owner got those—but still, it *almost* felt as if they were hanging up there. Maybe someday . . .

Just then she heard footsteps in the aisle outside. Glancing over her shoulder, she expected to see Miguel or one of the other grooms. But it was Fitz.

"What are you still doing here?" she asked in surprise. "I thought you went back to the hotel with the others."

"I did. But I came back." Fitz pulled a large, greasy white paper bag out from behind his back. "I wanted to celebrate your catch-riding awesomeness. I got your favorite—turkey on white and an orange soda."

"You brought me dinner?" Kate looked down at the bag as he handed it to her, touched by the gesture.

"I brought *us* dinner." He grabbed a show cooler that was hanging in the tack stall and spread it on the floor. "I knew you'd probably be too tired to go out, but I thought we could have a picnic. Just give me a sec . . ."

Soon the two of them were sitting down with sandwiches, chips, pickles, and sodas spread out between them. "Isn't this Summer's good cooler?" Kate said, fingering the edge of the monogrammed wool sheet. "She's going to be mad that we're getting it all dirty."

Fitz shrugged. "She'll never notice. It's not like she ever cools out her own horse. Besides, she's done for the weekend— I'm kind of surprised she's even sticking around to watch the eq, since she's not in it."

"She likes to keep track of what's going on." Kate picked a sliver of onion off her sandwich.

"Yeah, but who needs to be there in person now that we have that crazy blog?" Fitz rolled his eyes. "Anyway, let's not talk about Summer. Tonight's all about you and me. But mostly you." He smiled and raised his soda, clinking it against hers. "I'm really proud of you, you know. You were amazing out there."

"Thanks." She tilted her head playfully. "You really don't mind that I beat you?"

"I loved it. Keeps me in my place." He swigged his soda. "There's just one problem."

Kate reached for a handful of chips. "What?"

"Now it won't be such a surprise when you take the show world by storm next year." Fitz grinned. "I mean, you and Fable will definitely qualify for all the eq finals next season. Flame will be ready to show soon, plus I'm guessing after today you'll be getting more calls to catch-ride."

"Yeah." Kate stared at her food, suddenly realizing something. "Except . . ."

"What?" Fitz licked his fingers. "Hey, what's wrong? You look weird all of a sudden."

Kate shrugged. "I was just thinking about that rumor. You know, about Joy's job?"

"Oh right." Fitz smiled. "That's just one more piece of proof that you're the toast of the circuit these days."

Kate smiled weakly. "Yeah, except if I take the job, it will probably mean a lot less showing," she said. "I mean, that's kind of the whole point, right? Joy stays home and runs things there while Jamie's off at the shows."

"Oh." Fitz looked thoughtful. "I guess you're right. I never really thought about it that way." He reached over and rubbed a smudge of mustard off her chin, letting his thumb wander to her lower lip. "But Jamie wouldn't want to hold you back," he said, his voice suddenly husky. "I'm sure something will work out."

Kate closed her eyes as he leaned over the food and kissed her, trying to forget about that job, at least for now. Why let thoughts of the future ruin her perfect day?

FIFTEEN

"Who's Joy?" The girl with the wavy red hair looked distracted as she glanced at Zara over the rack of show shirts she was flipping through in one of the vendor booths.

"Joy—you know, the assistant trainer at Pelham Lane?" Zara watched the redhead's eyes carefully, but they were a blank. "There was some stuff about her on HorseShowSecrets last week."

"There was?" The girl shrugged, picking up one of the shirts for a closer look. "I guess I might have seen that. Is she the one who fell off that crazy jumper at Cap Challenge?"

Zara sighed, mentally checking another name off her list. "Never mind," she said. "I'll let you finish your shopping."

She hurried off without waiting for an answer. This whole detective deal was getting frustrating. The pieces just weren't fitting together—there was no way most of Zara's suspects could have found out all the gossip that had turned up on the blog.

And the news about Joy was the most perplexing of all.

Like the redhead, most of the juniors Zara had talked to had no clue who Joy was. So who could have found out her secret? Who would even care about something like that?

The answer was becoming clearer all the time. Pelham Lane.

Zara stopped in the middle of the aisle outside the vendor stalls, chewing the inside of her cheek. Could someone from her own barn really be the source of HorseShowSecrets? In one way, it made sense. Who else would bother to report the news about Joy? Some thirty-year-old lady getting pregnant wasn't exactly the type of hot gossip most juniors on the circuit would buzz about. Then there was the fact that Pelham Lane had appeared in the blog more often than any other barn— Zara's own research had shown that. She hadn't thought much about it at first, figuring it was just because it was one of the most successful barns out there. But now? She had to wonder.

Still, when she got right down to it, Zara couldn't figure out who it could be. Marissa was the most obvious suspect— everyone knew she was a huge gossip. But she also couldn't keep a secret to save her life. There was no way she could have been doing the blog all this time without someone finding out.

Fitz? Sure, he was the type who found it amusing to stir up trouble. But the boy was an open book, and besides, Zara was pretty sure he wouldn't keep stringing Kate along on this job rumor if he actually knew anything.

"Kate," Zara whispered as a new thought occurred to her.

Could *Kate* possibly be the blogger? Zara wandered along the curved and echoey aisleway, barely noticing the booths she was passing as she pondered her newest theory. Kate was always at the barn, always at the shows, always skulking around on the edges of things. She didn't usually have much to say, and Zara wasn't ever quite sure what the girl was thinking. Maybe she'd found out that Joy was leaving and started that rumor about taking over her job in the hopes of planting the idea in Jamie's mind. Stranger things had happened, right?

Zara sighed, shaking her head. On paper, it almost made sense. But when she thought about how uncomfortable Kate looked every time the topic of that job came up, she found it a lot harder to believe. Kate might be quiet and weirdly private, but she wasn't a sneak. Not like that. Besides, how would she find out about the hookups and other scandals at the different barns when she spent all her spare time working? Come to think of it, Zara wasn't sure Kate even had Internet access on her phone—so how could she post updates from the shows?

"Crap," Zara muttered, realizing she was running out of suspects. Who else was there? Tommi, Dani, Summer? Maybe some of the tweens that did the children's, or the younger juniors?

Zara stopped in front of a booth of custom oil paintings, staring at a big portrait of a foxhound without really seeing it. Tommi was easy to eliminate. No way would she put more gossip about herself out there. She got enough of that as it was, coming from the family she did. She and Zara had bonded over that more than once.

What about Dani and Summer, though? They both liked to gossip almost as much as Marissa did. The trouble was, Dani hadn't been at Cap Challenge, while the blogger had posted several tidbits from there. Come to think of it, she hadn't been to any shows for a while before that, either, thanks to that broken leg, and there had been plenty of updates about stuff that had happened at those shows.

As for Summer? Zara was skeptical. The girl was so self-absorbed that Zara couldn't imagine her bothering to post about anyone else. Especially people like Kate and Joy.

"Can I help you, dear?" The woman sitting in the booth stood and wandered toward Zara with a polite smile on her face. "That's a lovely piece, isn't it?"

Zara blinked, realizing she was still staring at the painting of the hound. "Uh, yeah," she said. "It's great. I've got to go."

She hurried on down the aisle, tempted to just give up on this whole stupid quest. After all, the rumor about Zac had blown over already; the tabloids had moved on to the scandal du jour. No harm done. Why not forget about it and enjoy the rest of the show?

Zara wandered toward the nearest entrance to the ring, where the Small Pony Hunters had started up a little while ago. She stood in the doorway staring at the tiny gray Welsh type zipping around the course.

"Hey," a voice broke into her thoughts. "We were looking for you."

It was Dani. "You found me," Zara said. "Where's everyone else? What have you guys been doing?" Most of Saturday's schedule didn't have much going on for the older juniors; just ponies and miscellaneous award ceremonies and stuff. Basically, they were all marking time until the main event tomorrow.

"Mostly studying." Dani shrugged. "But Mackenzie's up soon—we should try to catch her rounds."

Zara had only a vague idea of who Mackenzie was—Pelham Lane's pony kids all kind of looked alike to her. But she nodded and followed Dani into the arena.

Zara's barnmates had taken over a whole section of seats about halfway up. Summer was typing away on her laptop, while Marissa's schoolbooks were spread all over the seats in front of her.

"Ugh, homework." Zara glanced at Marissa's math book with a shudder. "Don't remind me."

She'd barely opened her books since arriving in Harrisburg, mostly because she'd been too busy with her investigation. Not that she needed much of an excuse to skip Spanish or algebra—or any other class, for that matter. Still. This stupid blog wasn't worth blowing her GPA, was it?

She flopped down beside Summer, leaning her chin on her hands and staring out at the ring. Nobody else seemed that interested in finding out who was writing the blog. At least not interested enough to do anything about it. So why did she care?

She had no clue. It wasn't like her to stick with something like this when it stopped being fun. Why bother? But this time, for some reason, she just wasn't sure she wanted to let it slide.

"More coffee, anyone?" The waitress paused beside the booth where Tommi was sitting with Marissa, Dani, Zara, and Fitz. The five of them had spent the past half hour chowing down on Mexican food and talking about tomorrow's eq finals.

"Not for me." Marissa put a hand over her cup. "I'll never fall asleep tonight if I have any more caffeine."

Tommi pushed her cup toward the waitress. "I'll take a refill, thanks."

"Getting jazzed up for your late-night schooling session?" Dani grinned at her across the table. "I get it. You don't want to look sleepy for Mr. Hot Stuff from California."

Tommi rolled her eyes, reaching for the sugar. "More like I don't want to *be* too sleepy to handle Fable."

"Uh-huh." Marissa smirked, trading an amused glance with Dani. "You're amazing, Tommi. I wish *I* had cute guys falling all over me everywhere I go."

Tommi ignored her, sipping the hot coffee. She was definitely planning to get some serious work done with Fable tonight. And if Scott happened to be there, too? Well, that was just a happy accident. Her only regret was mentioning it to Zara and the others, who hadn't let up on her all through dinner.

"By the way, I meant to ask earlier—where are Summer and Kate tonight?" she asked, hoping for a change of subject. "I tried to call Kate's room before I left to meet you guys, but there was no answer."

"Summer's having dinner with some relative who lives near here tonight," Marissa said.

"And I left Kate a note in our room." Dani glanced up from her food. "She didn't come back while I was getting changed. I figured she stayed behind at the show."

"She did." Fitz scooped up the last bite of his enchilada. "She wanted to stick around and help with feeding and stuff so Miguel can focus on getting the trailer gassed up and ready to head back tomorrow night."

"Really?" Tommi felt a pang of concern. For a while over

the summer, Kate had pretty much stopped eating. It had never quite turned into a real eating disorder as far as Tommi could tell, but she still kept an eye on her friend's food intake, especially during stressful times. "What's she going to do about dinner?"

"Already had it," Fitz said. "I picked up some nice greasy show food and ate with her while we watched the schooling rounds finish up."

"You mean this is your second dinner?" Zara stared at Fitz's plate, which was empty except for a few stray blobs of rice and salsa. "Gross."

Fitz just grinned at her. "Anyway, it sounds like Jamie wants us on the road as soon as possible after finals is done tomorrow night." He made a face. "For some reason he seems to think we all want to be super well rested for school on Monday."

"Ugh, I can't even think that far ahead." Tommi waved the idea away with one hand. "First I need to survive tomorrow."

"You'll be awesome." Zara raised her water glass in salute. "We'll totally be cheering you on. Right, guys?"

"Woo-hoo!" Dani whooped, pumping her fist. "Goooo Tommi!"

"Hey, what about me?" Fitz pretended to pout. "I'll be out there too, you know."

Marissa laughed. "Goooo Fitz!" she cheered.

"That's better." Fitz smiled, then leaned closer to Tommi, taking on a mock serious air. "So Tommi, tell us about this young man you're seeing tonight. What are his intentions?"

Tommi drained the rest of her coffee and slid out of the booth. "I think that's my cue to leave," she said, ignoring Marissa's giggles. "Someone cover me for dinner and I'll pay you back, okay? I want to get back over there and get ready to ride."

There were at least half a dozen other riders in the ring when Tommi rode in a few minutes before eleven, but her eyes went straight to the jet-black horse trotting along the opposite rail. Or, to be more accurate, that horse's rider.

Scott. Her gaze lingered on him for a moment, admiring the way he sat in the saddle like he belonged there. The coffee hadn't really kicked in yet and the heavy Mexican food had made her a little sleepy, but now she felt buzzed just watching him ride.

Then the black horse circled toward Tommi and she turned away, not wanting Scott to catch her staring. She let her gaze wander, taking in the rest of the place. She recognized most of the other horse-and-rider pairs as well—her competition for tomorrow. The stands were mostly empty, though a few die-hard juniors were still up there studying and one or two trainers were watching their students ride.

Tommi walked Fable along the rail, and a moment later heard hoofbeats. Scott pulled up beside her.

"Hey, you made it," he said. "I just got here too."

Tommi nodded, shortening her reins. As glad as she was to see Scott, she had to remember she wasn't here to flirt. She had work to do, and no guy—no matter how cute—was going to distract her.

"Fable's feeling good," she said with a smile. "I'd better get him moving."

"Cool. Ace is ready to go, too." Scott grimaced as his horse jumped to the side, almost crashing into Fable as another horse cantered past nearby. "Maybe a little too ready."

He pushed the black horse forward, trotting off before Tommi could respond. She watched for a moment, then nudged Fable into a trot as well.

For the next few minutes she almost forgot Scott was there as she and Fable did their thing. Almost.

After Fable cleared the big oxer at the end of their latest practice line, she brought him back to a walk and patted him. "Good boy," she murmured, feeling pleased with their progress. Considering she'd only ridden the horse a few times before this weekend, Tommi was feeling good about their chances tomorrow.

Once again, she found Scott riding up beside her. "Taking a walk break?" he asked. "Me too."

Tommi glanced over at his horse, Ace. "Your guy's a little spooky, huh? Has he been to Indoors before?"

"Nope." Scott grimaced. "It shows, huh? He did jumpers when he was younger, but he wasn't quite fast enough to bring it home in the jump-offs. For some reason my trainer thought he'd make a good eq horse, which is why I bought him. But I'm starting to wonder."

Tommi shrugged. "He got you this far, right? He must be pretty good."

"Yeah, I guess." Scott glanced at Fable. "So yours is a sale horse, huh? Is he young?"

"Not really. He's around nine or ten, I think—did the hunters for a while, but he's not a flashy enough mover to do that well." Tommi steered around a girl trotting past in the opposite direction. "So when his owners moved to Europe and left him with Jamie to sell, he convinced them Fable was perfect for the eq ring and they agreed. My friend Kate has been bringing him along all summer."

"Cool. And now here you are." Scott grinned. "Any chance you'll buy him if he gets you the win tomorrow?"

"What, you're actually admitting I'm going to beat you?" Tommi looked over with a sly smile. "About time you accepted the truth."

Scott laughed. "No way! I was just being polite. Seriously, though, you guys look good together. I just thought maybe you'd decide to add him to your barn on, you know, a more permanent basis."

Tommi kept her smile steady, but Scott's words had reminded her of her business plan. Other than looking at that one horse of Kara Parodi's, she hadn't really done anything about that yet. Sure, she could use Indoors as an excuse. But if she wanted to do this for real, she couldn't let any excuses stand in her way.

"Nah, not going to happen," she told Scott. "I'm happy with Orion—that's my eq horse, the one with the abscess. If I do the eq again next year, it'll be on him."

"If?" Scott raised an eyebrow.

Tommi shrugged. She hadn't really meant to say that. It was just something she'd been thinking about lately. If she wanted to get serious about training and selling horses, was there enough time to keep competing in all three rings? On the one hand, next season would be her last junior year—the one everybody talked about, the one that really counted. But most people ended up going off to college after that last hurrah, usually giving up riding and showing at least temporarily, if not forever. Tommi definitely wasn't planning to do that. So what was the big deal if she narrowed her focus a bit, dropped eq and just did hunters and jumpers next year? Those were the rings where she was most likely to find prospects for resale, and dropping the eq would give her more time to focus her business while still getting to show. Maybe that was more important than another year chasing points in the eq and trying to win finals.

But this wasn't the time to worry about that. She slid a challenging look at Scott. "Don't get your hopes up," she told him. "I'm definitely riding tomorrow, and that's all you should be worrying about right now."

Scott looked amused. "I'm thinking *you're* the one who should be worried. After all, you're the one on the new horse. What's his breeding like, anyway?"

"I'm not sure." Tommi swallowed a yawn as she tried to remember if Jamie or Kate had ever said anything about Fable's bloodlines. Her brain was feeling a little fuzzy around the edges—it had been a long day, and tomorrow would be even longer. "I'm pretty sure he's registered, though."

"Doesn't matter if they can do the job, right?" Scott said. "That's what my trainer always says."

"Jamie too." Tommi glanced down at Fable, who was wandering along with his neck stretched out and relaxed. "Guess we should get back to work, huh?"

Scott glanced around the ring. "I have a better idea."

"What?" Tommi couldn't help noticing that suddenly his expression looked oddly devilish.

"I don't see any trainers in here that I know, do you?"

Tommi scanned the arena. Several of the riders had left

while she and Scott were riding, leaving only three other horses besides theirs.

"I don't see any trainers in here at all right now," she said. "Why?"

"This could be our chance to see who's really the better eq rider." His voice held a definite challenge now. "Let's switch horses."

"Huh?" Tommi blinked, not sure she'd heard him right. "What are you talking about?"

"We'll probably have to do it tomorrow anyway as part of the final test if we both make the cut." Scott shrugged. "So let's get a sneak preview. You can hop on Ace here, and I'll take Fable for a spin. Come on, it'll be fun!" He grinned, raising his eyebrows. "Unless you don't have the guts?"

Tommi hesitated. She knew Jamie wouldn't approve if he were here. She was supposed to be using this time to get to know Fable better, not to ride random other horses.

But Scott was still staring at her with that challenging look in his eye. She couldn't let him think she didn't have the guts to ride his horse. No way.

"Sure," she said. "Let's do it."

"Great." Scott grinned and led the way to the middle of the ring, out of the way of the few remaining riders. "Need a leg up?"

Soon they were both mounted again. Scott's horse felt forward and very alert, but no worse than Toccata on a good day. Tommi didn't push the black gelding too hard—she trotted a few big, loopy circles and figure eights, just testing the controls. It was kind of fun—Ace was a very different ride from

Fable, and figuring him out actually made Tommi feel a little more awake.

After a few minutes she glanced around to see how Scott was doing. To her surprise, he had Fable going at a brisk canter, heading for a good-sized vertical. Tommi blinked in surprise. Sure, if the judge had them switch horses tomorrow they would have to jump, but somehow she'd assumed she and Scott were sticking to flatwork right now.

Fable pricked his ears at the jump, clearing it out of stride and landing well. Scott immediately turned and aimed the big gray at an oxer.

For a second Tommi felt a flash of unease. What if Scott really *was* trying to sabotage her? She'd heard of stranger things happening at finals. Maybe he'd lured her into liking him just so he could convince her to switch and let him wear out her horse, maybe crash him through a jump or two . . .

But once again, Fable jumped well, landed softly, and cantered away with his ears up. Scott brought him back to a trot, collecting the gait around the short end of the ring and then lengthening down the long side. Tommi relaxed, feeling foolish for her moment of panic.

"Come on, buddy," she said to the black horse. "If this is how we're playing it, I might as well see what you've got, too."

She spent the next few minutes testing all of Ace's buttons. He was solid at lateral work and transitions, but could be iffy when it came to collecting at the canter. And he refused to move past a particular mostly white banner at any gait without skittering away from it and tossing his head.

Overall, though, he was a lot of fun. And hey, it never hurt to ride other horses—that sort of thing could only help her eq, right?

Tommi brought the horse to a walk and patted him, glancing around for Scott. As she did, she noticed Kate standing at the rail near the gate. Probably stopping by to check on how Tommi was doing with Fable, maybe seeing if she needed any more tips to help get ready for tomorrow. Yikes. What was Kate thinking right now, seeing somebody else riding him?

Tommi felt oddly guilty, though she wasn't sure why. "Hey," she called to Scott, urging the black horse back into a trot to catch up with Fable. "Time to trade back. I need to finish schooling and get out of here before I fall asleep in the saddle."

Scott turned Fable into the center and pulled him up. "Okay, if you insist." He kicked his feet out of the stirrups and leaned forward to give Fable a pat on the neck. "But it was fun, right?"

"Sure." Tommi slid down from the black horse, quickly adjusting the stirrups back to Scott's length. "It was cool."

As she remounted, she sneaked a peek at Kate, who was watching with a puzzled expression. Oh well. Tommi would explain it to her later.

SIXTEEN

— — — — —

Kate bent to brush a stray bit of hay off Fable's legs. "Ready to tack up?" she asked Tommi, who was staring fixedly at the horse's broad hindquarters as she brushed the same spot over and over. "I'll go get your stuff."

"Thanks." Tommi continued brushing, even though the gray gelding's coat was already so clean you could eat off it. Kate and the grooms had seen to that, arriving even earlier than usual to make sure her and Fitz's horses were ready to go.

Kate hurried to the tack stall and grabbed Tommi's saddle. On the way back she passed Fitz, looking handsome in his tall boots and dark jacket. He was frowning and fiddling with his tie as he walked.

"Hey," he greeted Kate, one corner of his lip turning up in a half smile before his expression turned serious again.

"Hey," Kate replied. "I'll be over to help you tack up in a sec, okay?"

"Thanks." Fitz strode off without pausing for a kiss or a

flirtatious comment. That was unusual for Fitz, of course, but still not particularly surprising. Everyone in Pelham Lane's stabling area was very serious at the moment. No wonder. It was Medal Finals morning. This was the day Tommi and Fitz had worked toward all year.

When Kate got back to Tommi and Fable, Elliot was there. "I've got this," he said, reaching out to take Tommi's tack. "Why don't you go help Fitz. He's up before Tommi, and I think he's running behind as usual."

"Thanks." Kate patted Fable on the shoulder, then did the same to Tommi. "Good luck," she said. "We'll be out there cheering you on."

This time Tommi actually met her eye and cracked a tiny smile. "Thanks."

Soon Kate was back with Fitz, who had just set his saddle on his horse's back. Hastings was rock solid in the ring, but could be a bastard in the cross-ties. Fitz could handle that with a sense of humor most of the time, but at the moment he was cursing and scowling every time Hastings tried to nip him or lifted a hind foot as a warning.

"Here, let me do that." Kate stepped over to the horse's side. "You hold his head and distract him, okay?"

"Yeah. Okay." Fitz let her take the girth he was holding, then stepped to the horse's head. "Lay off, butt-head," he told the horse with a frown. "Can't you behave yourself for once in your life?"

"Be careful what you wish for," Kate said with a smile as she did up the girth. "If he did behave, we'd all be worried he was colicking or something."

"True." Fitz chuckled briefly. "Then I'd have to scratch, which I'm telling you, isn't seeming like the worst thing in the world at the moment."

Kate glanced at him. "You okay?"

"Not really." Fitz yanked at his tie, pulling it off-kilter. "You know, I don't remember being this nervous last year."

Kate finished tightening the girth, then dodged a nip from the horse as she stepped around his head to reach Fitz. "That's because you weren't one of the favorites last year." She pushed his hands away from his tie and straightened it. "But no pressure."

He caught her elbows, pulling her closer. "Maybe we should just run away right now." He bent his head closer until his breath warmed her hair. "Get out of here, hit the road, see the world."

"Sounds like fun." Kate slipped her arms around him, hugging him tightly. "But I'm thinking Jamie might not agree. You're supposed to meet him in the warm-up in like five minutes."

Fitz groaned, squeezing her back. "Do I have to?"

"Yes." Kate pulled back just enough to kiss him lightly on the lips. "And you're going to do great. I promise."

"Really?" He didn't sound completely convinced.

"Really." She smiled up at him. "You can do anything. I know you can."

"If you say so." He bent in for another kiss. "Okay, let's do it."

Kate pulled away, reaching for the bridle hanging nearby. Before she could pick it up, Fitz grabbed her hand, turning her toward him again. "What?" She glanced at the bridle. "We really need to get going. I wasn't kidding about Jamie and the warm-up."

"I know." Fitz smiled at her, squeezing her hand. "Just wanted to say thanks."

"You're welcome." Kate squeezed back, then dropped his hand. "Now let's go."

The warm-up went well, and before Kate knew it, she was giving Fitz's boots one last swipe with a rag to make sure they were spotless, and Jamie was at Hastings's head, rattling off last-minute instructions. A couple of the grooms were there, too—Miguel was dabbing a speck of green slime off the horse's mouth while Javier watched the rider currently in the ring. Then Kate heard Fitz's number come over the PA system and felt a shiver of nerves.

"Go get 'em," she said, reaching up and giving Fitz's knee a squeeze.

He smiled down at her, looking much calmer than he had earlier. "Thanks, babe. This one's for you." Then he glanced at Jamie, who was standing on the horse's other side, and laughed. "No offense, dude."

Jamie rolled his eyes. "Remember, don't cut the turn to the skinny too short," he said. "Now go!"

The gate swung open, and Fitz rode forward. Kate had to squint to keep her gaze on him against the bright arena lights.

She joined Jamie at the rail. The trainer's whole body was tense, and Kate knew better than to try to talk to him. So she just watched, holding her breath as Hastings cantered toward the first fence.

She wasn't sure she breathed again until after the last jump. Then she heard a loud whoop from beside her; Jamie was grinning now. Kate could hear cheers and whistles from the stands off to the left. She glanced that way and saw Zara, Marissa, and Dani doing what looked like an impromptu conga line in front of their seats, while Summer clapped politely nearby. The younger juniors were up there, too, along with some of the pony kids and their parents. Kate's heart swelled with pride for Fitz—and with gratitude for being part of such an amazing barn.

When she turned around again, the gate was swinging open to let Fitz exit. He had a grin on his face and was patting Hastings vigorously. The horse had his head up and his ears pricked, seeming to know he'd done well.

Kate smiled as she headed toward them. Amazing. And next year, if she worked hard and got lucky, that could be her out there, riding Fable in the finals. She shivered at the thought. Then she returned to the here and now as Fitz leaped out of the saddle, grabbed her, and swung her around until they were both dizzy and weak with laughter.

Tommi took a deep breath as she heard her number on the loudspeaker. She glanced down at Jamie.

"Ready?" he asked.

Tommi nodded. Jamie stepped back, Javier let go of Fable's bridle, and Tommi closed her legs to send the big horse forward. Fable's ears were pricked toward the collection of jumps in the ring as Tommi asked for a canter.

Fable leaped into it eagerly, building speed as they swooped around the edge of the course. Tommi half-halted, but the horse ignored her, ears swiveling as he took in the crowd and the ring and the rest of it. For a second Tommi wished she was on Orion; he'd been here before and wouldn't think twice about the electric atmosphere in the big ring.

But she shook the thought off immediately. No regrets. Fable could do this, and so could she. All she had to do was ride. She half-halted more firmly, and this time Fable responded, swiveling one ear back toward her as he shortened his big stride.

Tommi turned the horse toward the first jump, a heavily decorated vertical. Fable's ears pricked toward it, and for a second she felt him building speed again. This time when she steadied his stride he responded immediately. They hit their takeoff spot perfectly, sailing over the fence as if it were no more imposing than a crossrail.

The rest of the round went just as well. Fable overjumped a little at the Swedish oxer, but he ate up the rest of the jumps like a pro, extending or compressing his stride easily whenever Tommi asked. When they cleared the final jump, a cheer went up from the Pelham Lane section. Tommi knew they would have cheered for her even if she and Fable had knocked down every top rail and gone off course. But this time, she knew they deserved it. It had been a terrific first round. She wasn't sure if it was good enough for a top placing, but she was pretty sure they'd be called back for the second round at least.

"Thanks, buddy," she whispered, giving the big gray horse a pat as she rode out of the ring toward Jamie's waiting smile. "You were awesome."

Later, Tommi sat in the stands with her friends, watching Scott's ride. "He's looking good," Marissa commented as Ace cleared the first jump with a flourish.

"Trust me, Tommi knows how good that boy looks," Zara put in with a smirk.

Marissa laughed. "I was talking about the horse," she said. "I heard he's young and kind of green."

"He is. But he's talented, and Scott's definitely good enough to handle him." Tommi hadn't told anyone about that horse switch last night, and she was pretty sure Kate hadn't either.

"You have good taste in men, Tommi," Summer commented. "Everyone says Scott's one of the top ten this year for sure."

Tommi didn't respond. She held her breath as Scott and Ace made the sharp turn to the skinny jump, a narrow brick thing with no standards that had looked even narrower from horseback. Fable hadn't batted an eye at it, but Ace lifted his head as he cantered toward it. His stride faltered, and Tommi could see Scott urging the horse on.

"Oh!" Tommi's friends gasped along with most of the other spectators as Ace skidded to a stop a full stride out.

"Oh no," Tommi murmured, her heart breaking for Scott. There went his top-ten finish.

Scott spun the horse away, kicking him back into a canter and circling toward the jump again. But once again the horse refused, this time skittering sideways and tossing his head like a giraffe.

Tommi winced. Even from this distance, she could see that Scott's face was a frozen mask of frustration. This time he gave the horse a sharp smack with the crop as he circled away again. Scott didn't even try to maintain his perfect eq position as he cantered toward the skinny fence for the third time. He kicked, pumped with his arms, and used the crop again—and this time, finally, Ace popped over the jump, though it wasn't pretty.

The rest of the course was fine, though it was obvious that Ace was still rattled. Still, Tommi could see that Scott was trying to finesse the remaining jumps, make them look as good as possible. To salvage what he could after the disaster early on. She felt for him. It was exactly what she would have done in the same position.

As he and Ace headed for the gate at the end, Tommi stood. "I should go find him," she told her barnmates. "Say something nice. You know."

Dani scooted her legs to the side to let Tommi pass. Tommi hurried down the steps and back into the area behind the gate. There were dozens of people milling around back there, along with several horses. By the time Tommi pushed through the crowd, a groom was leading Ace away and Scott was nowhere in sight.

Tommi bit her lip, scanning the crowd for him. He'd probably hurried off with his trainer to talk about what had gone wrong. Maybe she should leave him alone for now. They could talk later.

"Man. I've never been so wiped on a show day when I didn't even ride!" Zara exclaimed. She was making her way down from their seats with Marissa, Dani, and Summer, heading for the barn area. The top four riders had finished their work-off, and the placings had just been announced.

"I can't believe Tommi came in ninth," Marissa exclaimed. "That's top ten!"

Zara shot her an amused look. "I can see all that studying you've been doing lately is paying off, Professor."

Marissa grinned. "You know what I mean. Tommi must be so psyched."

"Yeah," Dani agreed. "Fitz, too. Twelfth place isn't too shabby, right?"

Summer dodged a camera-wielding woman and nodded. "And both of them still have one more year, right?" she said. "They'll probably be, like, eq superstars next year. Especially since Tommi will be able to ride her own horse."

"Don't be dissing Fable," Zara said with a grin. "He was pretty amazing, especially for his first finals. By next year, he'll be even better—which means Kate will probably be right there battling it out with the other two in next year's work-off."

Marissa smiled. "Not bad for a barn that doesn't even focus on eq that much, right? Jamie is such a rock star, when you think about it."

Zara didn't answer, but she had to agree. When she'd come to Pelham Lane, Jamie hadn't impressed her much despite his stellar rep. He'd seemed too uptight, too strict, too whatever. Now? Maybe Zara was going soft, or maybe the party atmosphere in the arena was messing with her head. But she couldn't imagine going back to her old trainer from California, the one who'd pretty much let her do anything she wanted. That just didn't seem like so much fun anymore.

They'd reached ground level by then. Zara stood on her toes and craned her neck, trying to see over the heads of the people milling around everywhere. By then the grooms had led the horses off, leaving the human connections to celebrate. The whole place was abuzz with loud voices and laughter.

"I see them," Zara said. "Lucky Fitz is so tall—that big goofy head of his sticks up above almost everybody."

She led the way through the crowd, pushing past excited competitors and curious onlookers alike. Finally they reached the Pelham Lane group. Fitz had his arm slung around Kate's shoulders, and Tommi was talking a mile a minute to a smiling Jamie.

"Congrats, people!" Zara flung herself into the middle of the group, hugging Tommi first and then Fitz. "You guys were awesome!"

"Thanks!" Tommi's face was flushed, and her usual cool, calm, and collected exterior had given way to something that could almost be called giddiness. "I couldn't have done it without all of you!"

"You mean watching us show you how *not* to ride?" Marissa laughed, coming in for a hug. "You're welcome."

Tommi just grinned and hugged her. Jamie looked amused.

"Next year I expect to see you out there, Marissa," the trainer said.

Marissa's eyes widened with alarm. "Um, did I mention I might take up knitting? I'm very serious about it—it's probably going to take up all my time from now on."

Jamie chuckled as the rest of the juniors laughed. Then a wiry older woman came over and touched Jamie on the arm. Zara squinted at her. Why did she look so familiar?

"Sorry to interrupt, Jamie," the woman said, shooting a polite smile at the juniors gathered around the trainer. "But I know your juniors are shipping out tonight, and I was hoping to get things finalized before it got crazy."

"Uh-oh, business talk," Fitz whispered playfully to Zara

and the others. "Maybe we should leave Jamie alone. We can go ahead and start the party without him."

"Hold on," Zara murmured. She knew big-time trainers like Jamie did lots of business at shows. But this was kind of weird, wasn't it? What possible business discussion couldn't wait a few minutes, until Jamie had finished celebrating with his students?

Besides, she couldn't help noticing that Jamie had a slight frown on his face. "They're not leaving *that* soon, Sheila," he said. "Can I get back to you in a bit?"

Sheila? Wait, now Zara knew why the woman looked so familiar. She was one of the top trainers on the West Coast. Located up north near Los Altos somewhere, so Zara had only seen her at the bigger shows, but she knew her students won a lot.

"I'm sorry," Sheila was saying to Jamie. "But I'm sure you can understand how eager we are to get Fabelhaften settled in with us."

"Fable?" Zara blurted out. The other juniors had heard the name, too, and they all fell silent. "What's going on with Fable?"

Jamie sighed. "I'm sorry, guys," he said, his eyes seeking out Kate, who was huddled under Fitz's arm with a confused look on her face. "I didn't want to ruin the celebration by telling you right now. But Fable has been sold."

SEVENTEEN

Kate's whole body seemed to go hot and cold at the same time. She stared at Jamie, certain that she must have heard him wrong.

"What?" Dani exclaimed. "Fable's sold?"

Suddenly everyone started talking at once. Jamie held up a hand to quiet them, while the other trainer took a half step back, looking a little impatient.

"You all knew he was for sale," Jamie said. "I wasn't expecting him to sell this fast, but Sheila's client made an offer Fable's owners couldn't refuse. He'll be heading back to his new home in California after the show."

Kate could feel all eyes turn to her. "Oh, Kate," Tommi murmured.

Fitz was squeezing Kate's shoulders gently. "But this isn't fair," he said. "Kate put so much work into that horse—"

"Yes, I'm well aware of that, as are Fable's owners." Jamie's voice held an unmistakable warning, one not even Fitz could miss—his we'll-talk-about-it-later voice, as the juniors called it. "We all appreciate everything Kate has done to turn him into the horse we saw out there today."

Kate hardly heard him. She was still trying to take in this news. Fable was sold. He was gone—off to California to do the big eq with someone else. And unlike Tommi and Fitz, she didn't have a backup plan. There would be no fancy lease horse stepping in to take Fable's place. Just like that, Kate felt all her big eq dreams trickling away like the sad little fantasies they were.

"I'm sorry, Kate." Tommi was still watching her, looking miserable. "If I hadn't leased him for finals—" She cut herself off, blinking at something over Kate's shoulder.

Or some*one*, rather. When Kate turned, she saw that cute dark-haired guy coming toward them, the one Tommi had been flirting with lately—the one she'd let ride Fable last night. Kate couldn't remember his name, but she didn't really care right now.

"Hey, guys," he said. "Um, I guess you heard the news?"

Kate wasn't sure what he was talking about. But she saw recognition flash across Tommi's face, quickly followed by anger.

"You?" Tommi spat out. "*You're* the one who's buying Fable?"

Once again, everyone started talking at once. Kate couldn't listen anymore. What did the details matter? Fable was gone. That was how things worked when your only choice was to ride someone else's horses, and Kate knew that.

So why did it hurt so much?

Her lower lip trembled, and she realized she was losing it. Fitz must have felt it, because he looked down at her, his angry expression suddenly going soft.

"Come on," he said, tightening a protective arm around her. "Let's get out of here."

Kate didn't trust her voice to speak. She just nodded and allowed him to steer her away through the crowd as the tears started to flow.

"Look, Tommi. You know how stuff works."

Tommi glared at Scott. The two of them were behind a rack of T-shirts in one of the vendor stalls. Scott had dragged her there to talk while his trainer was working out the details with Jamie out by the gate.

"So you used me, basically." Tommi's voice was tight and hard. "Does that sum it up? You pretended to be interested in me just so you could check out Fable?"

She couldn't believe this was happening. It should have been one of the best moments of her junior career. Now? She could barely remember how happy she'd been just a few minutes earlier.

"That's not how it was, I swear." Scott took a step closer, his dark eyes troubled. "You have to believe me, okay? I mean, think about it—when we met at Cap Challenge, you were still riding your other horse."

Some tiny part of Tommi's brain was telling her that was true. But she ignored it.

"Big deal," she snapped. "So we flirted a little at Cap Challenge. That doesn't change what just happened." She couldn't believe she'd let herself get played like that. And she wanted to be a professional in this business? She'd definitely need to smarten up.

"I know you're probably really mad about that right now." Scott ran a hand through his hair, leaving it standing up in tufts. "But you'd do the same thing if it was the other way around—I know you would."

"No, I wouldn't," Tommi retorted.

He didn't look convinced. "You saw my horse out there today. He's talented, but way too spooky for the eq. And I only have one year left to try for finals—I want to make the most of it. I *know* you understand that."

Tommi just shrugged, not willing to concede anything.

"So my trainer and I have been looking for something that could take me to the top next year, and that's Fable." He stared at her as if willing her to agree, to understand. "I knew it when I saw you on him that first time, and I was even more sure when I sat on him last night."

Tommi cringed. "You definitely used me there," she said. "Now I know why you were asking so many questions about Fable. I thought it was . . ." She didn't bother to finish. It was embarrassing enough that they both knew what she'd been about to say. She'd thought he was interested in *her*, not her mount. She'd thought it was just more flirting. "Now I know why you were so eager to switch horses," she finished instead. "That was low."

"Maybe a little." Scott looked chastened. "But I swear to you, Tommi, this whole Fable deal doesn't have anything to do with you and me. I thought you were cool from the start, okay? That's the only reason I even noticed Fable."

That definitely didn't make Tommi feel any better. She flashed back to the wounded look on Kate's face. Fable had been her big chance—her best shot at winning one of those eq finals next year. Now that shot was gone, and it was all Tommi's fault.

"I've got to go," she muttered, turning away from Scott. She felt his hand on her arm, but shook it off. "Have a nice life."

"At least this makes one thing easier." Kate pressed her back against the cool wall behind her. She and Fitz had escaped from the main ring; now they were huddled in an out-of-the-way spot in the hallway outside. Fitz was holding both her hands and watching her closely.

"What?" he asked.

Kate met his concerned gaze for a moment before looking away again. "Since it turns out I won't be doing the eq next season, there's really no reason not to take that job if Jamie offers it. Even if it means staying home from all the shows."

"Who says you won't be doing the eq?" Fitz squeezed her hands. "Fable's not the only eq horse in the world, you know. Or even in the state of New York."

Kate felt weary, wishing that for once she didn't have to explain it to him. How her life was very different from his, in lots of important ways he seemed not to notice most of the time.

"It doesn't matter how many eq horses are out there," she said. "Without Fable's owners footing the bills, there's no way I can afford to get anywhere near a big eq class again."

Fitz still looked unconvinced. "You don't know that. Maybe Jamie will get in another horse for training or something."

Kate shook her head. This time she didn't bother to respond, letting Fitz figure it out for himself. Jamie wasn't an eq trainer—not really. Yes, some of his students did the big eq, and some even did it well enough to keep up with the kids from the eq specialist barns—Tommi and Fitz had just proved that. But Jamie wasn't going to start focusing on eq sales just for Kate's benefit. Most of his sale horses were hunters or jumpers. Even Fable had started out that way.

Fitz was frowning as he dropped her hand to wipe a stray tear off her cheek with his thumb. "Anyway, eq's not the only game in town, right? Maybe this is a good thing—it means you can focus all your talent on taking Flame to the top instead. I bet you guys will be tearing up the hunter ring at Indoors next year."

"Maybe." Kate didn't even try to sound hopeful. "But who knows if he'll have what it takes?"

"He will." Fitz's optimism was sounding slightly desperate now. "He does. You said so, remember?"

Kate shrugged. "We'll see. But I can't let that affect my decision about the job thing. I can't pin my hopes on one horse, especially one that belongs to someone else." She shot Fitz a look. "Even if that someone is you."

Fitz frowned for a second, as if he was about to argue with what she'd just said. Then he shrugged. "Anyway, lots of people make it to eq finals. How many get hired to help manage a barn like Pelham Lane at age sixteen?" He smiled down at her. "It just proves what I've always thought—you're one of a kind, babe."

Kate smiled back, but her stomach clenched as she thought about what he'd just said. It was one thing to have her own mind made up about that job. But how in the world was she going to break the news to her parents that she was dropping out of high school?

Oh well. She would figure it out. It wasn't as if she had much choice, right?

That thought was depressing. Kate had never been a fan of difficult decisions, but maybe it was better to have hard choices than none at all. Or was it? She'd spent every day since that blog post came out wondering what to do if Jamie offered her Joy's job. Worrying that taking over the assistant trainer position would mean giving up on her own dreams of showing. Now the choice had been made for her. She could stop worrying about it.

At that moment Marissa hurried around the corner. She skidded to a stop when she saw Kate and Fitz. "There you guys are," she said breathlessly. "The horses are loaded, and Elliot already left with the trailer. Miguel's pulling the van around to pick us up right now."

Kate dropped Fitz's hands and straightened up, glancing toward the entrance to the main ring. Even though junior weekend was over, the show had another week to run; Jamie was staying to do the professional and adult divisions, starting with several rides in the First and Second Year Greens the next day. But the juniors were heading home, and Kate felt a weirdly intense flash of nostalgia. Would she ever set foot in the show ring here again?

She had no idea. But she knew one thing. Her show was over. It was time to go home.

EIGHTEEN

——— ——— ——— ——— ———

Zara propped her legs up against the seat in front of her and stared out at the highway lights flashing by. Jamie's old but comfortable GMC passenger van was cruising up Interstate 78 a few car lengths behind Jamie's largest trailer. They'd caught up to it just a few miles outside Harrisburg, even though Elliot had pulled out of the show a good half hour before them. No surprise there. Elliot drove like someone's grandma, especially when he was hauling horses.

Miguel had the van's radio tuned to a Spanish music station; when Dani complained, the groom had reminded her that only the driver got a vote. After that, everyone had talked about the show for a while, but it had been pretty clear that both Kate and Tommi were uncomfortable anytime the conversation strayed too close to the eq finals in general or Fable in particular. Eventually everyone had gone quiet, and now the mood in the van was sleepy and a little somber.

Zara yawned, leaning her forehead against the cool glass of the window. She couldn't believe Harrisburg was over already. Even though she and Ellie had managed not to embarrass themselves in the ring, Zara felt oddly guilty, as if she'd done something wrong. Probably because she hadn't figured out the blogger's identity as she'd vowed to do.

She tried to shake off the feeling. Since when did she even want to be Nancy Drew? Everyone knew that girl was a goody-goody who liked to stick her nose into everyone else's business.

"So I still can't believe I didn't pin in a single over-fences class," Summer spoke up suddenly, her voice peevish and too loud in the silence. She turned and looked back from the front passenger seat, which she always insisted on hogging by claiming she got carsick if she sat in the back. "I swear, I think my horse is trying to make me look bad sometimes."

"Win some, lose some." Fitz was sitting with Kate and Tommi in the middle seat. "There's always next year."

"Maybe." Summer stared from him to Tommi and back again. "But I'm thinking maybe the hunters isn't really my thing. I'm going to talk to Jamie about finding me an eq horse."

Zara rolled her eyes. Leave it to Summer to blame her lack of ribbons on her very nice small junior hunter instead of her own tendency to slow him to a crawl in the last few strides anytime she couldn't see her spot. If she thought things were going to be any easier in the eq, where all eyes were on her and her riding, she was in for a rude awakening.

"Too bad you didn't decide this yesterday." Zara didn't even try to keep the sarcasm out of her voice. "Maybe you could've bought Fable instead of that Scott guy."

Summer frowned at her. "Maybe I could have."

Tommi let out a snort. "Yeah, right."

"What?" Summer stared at her, a mulish look coming over her face. "You don't think I could afford him?"

"Oh, I'm sure you could *afford* him." Tommi sounded cranky. "But he's not a packer like your poor patient horse, you know. Kate just made him look that way."

"So did you, Tommi," Marissa put in quickly, obviously trying to smooth things over before the conversation degenerated into more sniping. "You can't blame anyone for thinking Fable's a dream ride after those trips you laid down with him today."

Tommi shrugged and looked down at her hands, but Summer didn't seem pacified. "Anyway, if I had tons of extra coaching from Jamie all the time like *some* people, I'm sure I could ride a horse like that, too."

This time Summer's glare was directed at Kate. "Whatever," Dani said. "I'm sure Jamie can find you an eq horse if you're serious about it."

"Of course I'm serious. Why wouldn't I be serious?" Summer frowned at her.

"Um, because you just came up with this idea like five minutes ago?" Dani said.

Summer scowled at her. "What do you know, Dani? You don't even do the eq, so stay out of it."

She spun around in her seat and stared out the front window, her pout reflected for all to see. Dani just snorted, speechless for once. Zara closed her eyes, suddenly tired of all the drama.

"Wake me up when we get home, okay?" she said.

Tommi had barely set foot in Drummond's lobby the next morning when she heard someone calling her name.

"Oh my god, Tommi, welcome back," Court exclaimed, rushing over. "You'll never believe the party you missed this weekend, or who was there acting like she—wait, are you okay?"

She peered into Tommi's face with sudden concern. "I'm fine." Tommi pasted on a smile.

"Does this mean you didn't win your big championship thingy?" Court fell into step beside Tommi, both of them heading toward the hall where their lockers were located.

"No, I did fine. Really well, actually." Tommi shrugged. "Ninth out of like two hundred and fifty in the eq."

"Wow." Court looked impressed. "So what's with the face?"

Tommi hesitated. Court was one of her best friends, and normally she would probably be the first to hear about the disaster with Scott. Somehow, though, Tommi just wasn't in the mood to get into it right now.

"Nothing," she said, forcing another smile. "I'm just tired. Didn't get in until really late, and it's not like I'm looking forward to that calc test today."

Court barked out a laugh. "Tell me about it! My eyes were crossing trying to cram for that thing last night."

"So what's this about a party?" Tommi asked.

Court's face lit up. "Oh man, it was legendary . . ." She started chattering on about the party, though Tommi wasn't really listening. Her mind drifted back to Scott. He'd sent her a text last night, trying again to apologize for what had happened, insisting again that the thing with Fable hadn't had anything to do with her.

Could he be telling the truth? Tommi thought back to what

he'd said yesterday—that she would have done the same thing if the situation were reversed. At first Tommi had dismissed that. But she'd had lots of time to think about it on that long, mostly quiet ride back to New York last night, and now she wasn't so sure.

What *would* she have done differently, after all? What if Scott had been riding a promising young prospect—one that could have been a match for Tommi's business plans, one that was for sale at a fair price? She would have jumped at the chance, even if it meant being a little cagey. Right? It would have been stupid to do otherwise. So maybe he was right. They really weren't so different.

Of course, that didn't make Tommi feel much better about what had happened. Or any less guilty every time she thought about Kate . . .

"Tommi!" Zara's excited voice broke into Tommi's thoughts—and Court's story.

Court frowned slightly. "Hi, Zara," she said in her legendary blow-off voice. "Look, Tommi and I are right in the middle of—"

"Not interested." Pushing past Court, Zara grabbed Tommi by the arm. In her other hand, she was clutching her phone. "Tommi, I need to talk to you about something. Right now."

Tommi could see that the HorseShowSecrets blog was on the phone's screen. She frowned. "Can it wait? I'm not really in the mood for—"

"This can't wait." Zara yanked impatiently on her arm. "I mean it, girl. I've got to show you something—*now.*"

Kate was late arriving at the barn on Tuesday afternoon because Mr. Barron had insisted that she stay after school to take the quiz she'd missed on Friday. Kate had tried to explain that she was supposed to work every day after school, but when he'd started talking about calling her parents to discuss whether her schedule was too demanding, she'd given in and agreed to stay.

The parking area wasn't very full. Most of the adult riders wouldn't be out this week, since their horses were at the show. As Kate pulled into her usual spot, she saw that Tommi and Dani were already there, though there was no sign of Fitz's car. Kate hadn't heard from him all day, and she hoped he hadn't forgotten that the juniors had a lesson that afternoon. Joy might be an easier teacher than Jamie in some ways, but she was just as strict when it came to expecting everyone to be on time. Kate glanced at her watch. Come to think of it, she would have to hurry if she wanted to get anything done before it was time to start tacking up.

She cut her engine and just sat there staring into a space for a moment, realizing that she'd almost added one more word to the last part of that thought: before it was time to start tacking *Fable* up. For the past few months, she'd ridden the big gray gelding in most of her lessons. It was going to feel weird to go back to switching back and forth onto whichever horse Jamie thought needed more schooling that week.

Kate closed her eyes for a second as an intense feeling of loss washed over her. Not just the loss of Fable—she'd always known he wasn't really hers. She just hadn't expected him to go so soon. More importantly, she hadn't recognized until too late how tied in he was with her hopes for the future.

Shaking her head to clear out those kinds of thoughts,

Kate yanked the key out of the ignition, grabbed her boots, and headed inside.

Tommi was perched on the bench in the entryway, fiddling with the laces on her paddock boots, when Kate entered. "Oh, hi," she said, glancing up. "Joy asked me to tell you to come see her when you get here."

"Didn't she get my text saying I'd be late?" Kate said with a flash of panic. The last thing she needed to do right now was make Joy and Jamie think they couldn't rely on her.

Tommi gave her laces one last yank and straightened up. "She didn't say anything about that. She didn't seem mad or anything, though."

Kate nodded and relaxed, belatedly remembering that the assistant trainer had responded to that text, saying it was no problem if she was a few minutes late. So what was this about?

"I'd better go find her," she told Tommi. "See you at our lesson."

Joy was in the office when Kate peeked in, poring over some paperwork. At Kate's soft knock on the doorframe, the assistant trainer looked up with her usual cheerful smile.

"Kate!" she said. "How was your quiz?"

"Fine," Kate lied. "Tommi said you wanted to see me?"

Joy pushed back from the desk and stood. If Kate hadn't been watching so carefully, she might not have noticed that the assistant trainer was moving a little more carefully than normal.

"Follow me." Joy brushed past Kate. "Something came for you this morning."

Confused, Kate trailed behind Joy as she hurried down the aisle to the tack room. "Something came for me? What do you mean—like a letter or something?"

"It's from Fable's owners," Joy explained. "A gift to thank you for the work you put into him?"

"Really?" Kate was touched and surprised. "Wow, they didn't have to get me anything. That's really nice of them."

"No kidding." Joy grinned, leading the way into the tack room. "Voilà!"

At first Kate didn't understand. Joy was gesturing toward a saddle sitting on the stand in the center of the room. It looked a lot like Tommi's best saddle, except that there were no wear marks from the stirrup leathers on the flap.

"What do you think?" Joy was still grinning as she stepped over and patted the soft leather of the saddle. "They said if it's the wrong size, you can exchange it."

Kate gasped as she realized what Joy was saying. "Wait," she said. "They got me a *saddle*?"

"A nice one, too." Joy ran her fingers over the pommel. "County, which makes me think Jamie must've told them which of his extra saddles is your favorite to ride in." She winked. "Brand-new, though, unlike Jamie's dinosaur. The guy from the tack shop dropped it off about an hour ago."

Kate couldn't answer. Couldn't do anything but stare at the saddle. Was this really happening? There had to be some mistake. Fable's owners hadn't actually bought her a *saddle*, had they?

"Wanted to make sure you saw it before you start tacking up for the lesson, since I'm sure you'll want to break it in." Joy checked her watch. "Speaking of which, I'd better finish that grain order before it's time to start. Feel like taking Jupiter for a spin today?"

"Huh? Um, sure." Kate wasn't really thinking about the

spunky large pony, one of her favorite rides before Fable had come along. She was staring at the saddle—*her* saddle—trying to comprehend the idea that she could own something so nice.

As Joy hurried out, Kate cautiously put one hand on the seat. The leather was buttery soft and smooth.

Just then Marissa and Dani hurried into the tack room, chattering about the lesson. "Hey, Kate," Marissa said. "What's up?"

"Nothing." Kate cleared her throat, a little worried that she was about to start laughing hysterically. "Um, except that Fable's owners sent me a saddle."

Dani's eyes widened as she glanced at the saddle Kate was caressing. "Whoa! Really? What kind is it?" She grabbed the flap, flipping it up to check out the name printed on the panel underneath. "Nice!"

"What a sweet gift," Marissa added. "The Langleys seemed like really nice people—I'm not surprised they wanted to thank you for helping them with Fable."

Just then Fitz stuck his head into the room. "Am I late?" he asked.

"Get in here, dude." Dani grinned at him. "I'm thinking you're going to have to start buying your girlfriend much nicer gifts if you want to keep up."

"What?" Fitz sounded confused. "Gifts? What are you talking about?"

"Check it out—Fable's owners gave Kate a saddle!" Dani waved a hand at the saddle.

"Oh!" Fitz stepped inside. "Really? That's great, babe. You earned it."

"I—I don't know." Kate gulped. "Can I really accept something like this?"

"Sure, why not?" Fitz walked over to check out the saddle. "It's a gift. It'd be rude *not* to accept it." He glanced up with a grin. "At least, that's what my mom tells me every time my crazy great-aunt Phyllis sends me another ugly sweater."

Marissa laughed. "Are you going to ride in it today, Kate?"

"Duh!" Dani stepped over and grabbed her bridle off the wall. "Of course she's going to ride in it! Why would she ride in one of Jamie's thousand-year-old spares when she could ride in *that*?"

Tommi hurried into the room, followed by Summer. "I'm serious, Tommi," Summer was saying. "If you see any good eq horses for sale while you're looking for prospects and stuff, let me know."

"What's going on?" Tommi asked, surveying the room and ignoring Summer.

Everyone started talking at once, filling her in. Well, everyone except Kate. She just stared at the saddle in wonder.

"Whoa," Tommi said when she caught on. "That's awesome, Kate! Congratulations—you definitely deserve it."

"It's a County?" Summer sniffed and turned away. "Too bad they didn't get you a French saddle—they're much nicer."

"Is that right?" Tommi said with a slight smile. "Hmm, guess I missed that memo."

"Oh, I wasn't talking about *your* saddle, Tommi," Summer said hurriedly. "Um, I mean, if you have a County, I'm sure they're really nice."

At any other time, Kate might have laughed. Leave it to Summer to accidentally insult Tommi while acting snooty toward Kate. Right now, though, she wasn't really focused on anything except trying to accept that this was really happening.

Just then Zara stepped into the tack room. Marissa waved to her. "Check this out, Zara," she said. "Kate got a new saddle."

"Really? That's nice." Zara barely glanced at the saddle before her eyes swept around the room. "Is everyone here? Good. Because I have something to tell all of you."

"Bad timing." Marissa grinned. "We're too busy drooling over Kate's new County."

Zara pulled out her phone and held it up. The HorseShowSecrets logo was gleaming out from the tiny screen.

"I think you guys are going to want to hear this," she said. "I finally figured out who's behind the blog."

NINETEEN

— — — — —

Zara smiled at the looks of surprise and curiosity on everyone's faces. Well, everyone except a couple of people. One was Tommi—she already knew what Zara was going to say, of course. As for the other person . . .

"Seriously?" Summer exclaimed. "Who is it?"

"Yeah, spill." Fitz looked excited. "Don't keep us in suspense!"

"Don't worry, I won't." Zara surveyed the room. "See, I figured it out when I saw what was posted on HorseShowSecrets first thing yesterday morning."

"What was it?" Marissa pulled out her phone, quickly pulling up the blog and scrolling through it. "Not the thing about the weirdo from Kentucky with the horseshoe fetish?"

"Nope. The post before that." Zara glanced at her own phone. "See? It talks about how Pelham Lane did so great at Medal Finals. . . ."

"'And they might do even better next year, since at least

one more junior from that barn was inspired to start shopping for an eq horse so she can go for it next season,'" Marissa quoted from the blog. She looked up. "They must mean Summer, right?"

"Right." Zara glanced at Summer, who looked as perplexed as the rest. "But how could someone find out she said that? Only the seven of us were there to hear her say she wanted to start doing the eq."

"Wait." Summer frowned as several people turned to stare at her. "*I'm* not writing the blog, if that's what you're thinking. I swear!"

"I know," Zara said. "I'm not accusing you of anything."

Marissa looked confused. "So then who was it—Miguel?"

"Yeah, right. I'm sure Miguel's totally using all his free time blogging." Fitz grinned. "I can picture it now."

"It's not Miguel," Tommi said quickly.

Summer turned toward her. "Do you know what she's talking about?"

Tommi just shrugged and raised an eyebrow at Zara. Okay, Zara might not be a professional actress like her mother, but she could pick up a cue.

Now she just had to hope that the guilty party could, too. As satisfying as it had been to solve the mystery, Zara wasn't sure she had the stomach to actually out someone. Not now that she knew who it was.

"Tommi's right, it's definitely not Miguel," she said. "Or Summer, either. But the blogger is in this room right now."

"Huh?" Fitz stared around, looking confused.

"Zara, what are you—" Marissa began.

Before she could finish, Dani stepped forward, swallowing

hard. "She's right, guys," she said, her voice shaking a little. "It, uh, was me."

"You?" Summer shrieked. "Oh my god, Dani!"

"I'm really sorry." Dani twisted the bridle she was holding in both hands. "I never meant for it to cause so much trouble. I was just really bored and lonely and missing the barn after I broke my leg. My parents wouldn't let me go anywhere or do anything fun, so I started the blog. You know, to sort of stay connected to the show world while I was out of commission."

"Wait," Fitz said. "This doesn't make sense. Like you said, you were stuck home with a broken leg—so how could you post stuff from shows you didn't even go to?"

"Like Cap Challenge, for one," Kate put in.

Dani shrugged and sneaked a guilty look at Marissa. "I got the gossip from various sources," she said. "Um, mostly Marissa, when it came to the stuff about you guys."

"You mean you two were working together?" Fitz asked.

"No!" Marissa and Dani said at the same time.

"I didn't know anything about it," Marissa added with a frown at Dani.

"She really didn't." Dani bit her lip. "I'm sorry, M. At first I didn't say anything because it was just for fun, you know? I figured I'd tell you guys when I got back here. But then the blog caught on and everybody was talking about it, and well . . ." She shrugged helplessly. "Things sort of got out of control."

Yeah, no kidding. Zara felt a flash of anger when she thought about that rumor about her father. Not to mention some of the other stuff that had been posted about her and her friends. And of course if it wasn't for that freaking blog, maybe she and Marcus would still be on speaking terms . . .

She shook her head, trying not to think about that.

"So you actually did it." Fitz turned to Zara, looking impressed. "You cracked the secret."

"Yeah. I figured even Summer wouldn't have had time to blab about her new eq dreams before school started on Monday." Zara shrugged. "And when I remembered how Dani's always texting people at other barns, it was pretty easy to figure it out."

Tommi was staring at Dani. "So what are you going to do now?" she asked. "You wrote a lot of messed-up stuff on that blog."

"I know." Dani looked abashed. "I'm really sorry, guys. I never meant to hurt anyone." She looked uncomfortable. "I guess I have to confess to everyone else too, huh?"

At that moment Joy stuck her head into the room. "Why are you all standing around?" the assistant trainer said. "Is my watch wrong, or aren't you all supposed to be meeting me in the indoor in less than twenty minutes?"

"Sorry, Joy." Casting one more frosty look at Dani, Marissa hurried over and took her bridle down from the wall. "We were just going to start tacking up."

"Right." Fitz reached for his bridle, too. "Come on, Kate. Grab that gorgeous new saddle of yours and let's go."

Soon everyone was collecting their tack and scurrying out of the room. Zara followed more slowly. She'd done it. She'd solved the mystery, done what she set out to do, righted a wrong.

So why did she feel kind of let down?

"How's the saddle?" Tommi stopped her horse beside Kate's.

Kate glanced down at the pommel of the new County. *Her* new County. She couldn't quite get used to that thought.

"Amazing," she admitted. "The leather's so nice it's like it doesn't even need to be broken in." She hesitated. "But I still feel a little weird about, you know, accepting it as a gift or whatever. I mean, these saddles are really expensive."

"Don't worry about that." Tommi turned to watch Fitz jump through the gymnastic Joy had set up in the center of the ring. "If you were a pro instead of a junior, you'd probably be getting a share of the commission on Fable's sale. And that would be a lot more money than any saddle costs."

Kate didn't respond. It was easy for Tommi to talk about this stuff so casually. She owned at least three or four nice saddles. How could she possibly understand how weird this was for Kate—knowing her new saddle was worth more than most of the people in her neighborhood brought home in two or three paychecks?

"Kate!" Joy's voice broke into her thoughts. "Wake up, darling. Your turn."

"Sorry." Kate gathered her reins and nudged Jupiter forward.

By the end of the lesson, she'd regained her focus. Jupiter, another sale horse, had been a lot of fun to ride, even though Joy had told her she hadn't had time to do more than lunge the always-energetic pony since the previous week.

"Go ahead and cool out, guys," Joy called, already heading for the gate. "I've got to go. Text me if you need me."

She hurried out. "Bet we all know where she's going, thanks to a certain blog I could mention," Marissa said as soon as the assistant trainer was out of earshot.

"Yeah." Fitz grinned. "She's got an appointment with the porcelain god."

"Ew." Summer made a face. "Being pregnant sounds gross."

That made everyone laugh, although Kate noticed that Dani's giggle sounded a bit forced. She'd been pretty subdued during the lesson, too. No wonder. Kate still couldn't quite believe she'd been behind the blog all along.

"Listen, guys," Dani spoke up hesitantly as they all walked their horses around on a loose rein. "I want to make things right. How about pizza after the lesson—my treat?"

Kate traded a look with Tommi. In the summer, the juniors ordered pizza after just about every group lesson. Things were more rushed during the school year, so it had been a while since they'd had a chance to enjoy that particular tradition.

"Sure," Tommi spoke up first. "That sounds like fun. Thanks, Dani."

"Yeah, free slices are always a good thing," Fitz added. "I'm in."

"Me too," Summer said.

"Cool." Dani looked relieved. She cast a cautious look at Kate and Marissa. "What about you guys?"

"I said I'd help Joy and Max bring horses in from turnout after the lesson," Kate said. "But I'll come by when I'm done. Thanks, Dani."

Marissa shrugged, not meeting Dani's eye. "If everyone else is going, I guess I will too."

Kate winced at the hard tone in her voice, so unlike Marissa's usual sweet attitude. It seemed maybe Marissa wasn't quite ready to forgive Dani, even if everyone else was.

Surprising—or maybe not. On the one hand, Marissa was

one of the most easygoing people Kate knew. And Dani had never written anything rude, scandalous, or untrue about Marissa on the blog, as far as Kate had noticed. On the other hand? She'd used one of her best friends as a source without telling her. Now that Kate thought about it, she guessed that might make it hard for Marissa to trust Dani again.

Come to think of it, Kate was pretty sure that was how Nat saw the thing between the two of them. A breach of trust. Kate going behind her back to take advantage of her.

Not that it had really happened that way. Still. She wondered if Nat would ever forgive her—if things would ever go back to the way they were. How could they, after the terrible things Nat had said—the rumors she'd started, the wild accusations? Did Kate even *want* to be friends with her anymore?

She knew what Tommi would say, or Zara. They would tell Kate to kick Nat to the curb and forget about her.

But it wasn't that easy. How could she just forget about a lifelong friendship? After all, nobody was perfect. Right?

She was still thinking about it a few minutes later as she led Jupiter into his stall. When she returned to the grooming area to grab her saddle—*her* saddle!—everyone else had disappeared, but Fitz was there waiting.

"Pizza's not here yet," he said. "But that's okay—I was hoping to catch you."

Kate grabbed her saddle and the bridle she'd used in the lesson, then straightened up and studied Fitz. "What's going on?" she asked. "You look weird."

"Just what every guy wants to hear from his girlfriend." Fitz grinned. "But listen, I have a surprise for you. It's sort of a way to make you feel better about what happened with Fable. Wait here a sec, okay?"

"Um, sure," Kate said, although he was already halfway down the aisle.

She set her saddle down and waited. What was Fitz up to now? Was this another of his sweet, romantic gestures, like that picnic at the show? Okay, probably not a picnic, since the pizza would be there soon . . .

She hadn't figured it out yet when she heard hoofbeats at the end of the aisle. "Close your eyes!" Fitz yelled. "Are they closed?"

"Yes." Kate closed her eyes, smiling slightly. Was he about to whisk her off on a romantic moonlight trail ride or something? If so, she could only hope he'd cleared it with Joy first—and that it wouldn't take too long. Maybe if she skipped the pizza, she could get everything done at the barn and still be home in time to finish those chemistry proofs she'd started in study hall.

"Okay." Fitz's voice sounded much closer now, and Kate could hear a horse breathing and shifting its weight. "You can open your eyes."

Kate did so. Then she blinked. Fitz had led Flame into view. He wasn't tacked up, but he did have an enormous, floppy bow tied around his neck in bright purple ribbon.

"Surprise!" Fitz exclaimed.

Kate patted Flame, who was stretching his nose toward her. "Okay," she said. "Um, I don't get it."

"I'm gifting you half ownership in our boy here." Fitz grinned. "Flame's half yours now, baby!"

"What?" Kate rolled her eyes. "Yeah, right. Very funny."

"No, I'm serious." Fitz handed her the lead line. "I mean, it makes sense, right? We've been partners in this guy from the start—I'm just making it official. Call it an early six-monthiversary gift if you want."

Kate shook her head, waiting for the punch line. Because this had to be some weird Fitzian joke, right?

Then again, maybe not. Now that she thought about it, this was just crazy enough to be a real Fitz idea.

"You can't be serious," she said hesitantly. "I mean, you can't do that, can you? Just—just *give* someone half of a horse."

"Sure you can. Why not?" He shrugged. "People do it all the time. Some racehorses are owned by a whole group of people."

"But . . ." Kate wanted to argue, but she recognized that look in Fitz's eye. He was serious about this. No matter how crazy it seemed, he really was giving Flame to her—well, half of him, anyway. She stared at the horse, who was arching his neck as he tried to nibble at his bow. She'd ridden more horses in her life than she could count, but she'd never owned one. Never even *dreamed* of owning one as special as Flame. "It's too much!" she blurted out. "You can't—I can't—"

"Can. Did. Already started the paperwork." Fitz grinned. "And remember what I was saying earlier? You can't turn down a gift. It's totally rude."

That reminded Kate of the saddle. "I could give you this," she blurted out, reaching down to paw at it. "I know it probably wouldn't pay for the whole thing, but—"

"No thanks. I already have enough saddles. Besides, you'll need a nice saddle to use when you and Flame make it to the show ring." Fitz stepped over and grabbed the saddle. "Let's see if it fits him."

He set Kate's saddle onto Flame's bare back. The horse stood quietly as Fitz stepped around him, examining the fit from every angle.

"Perfect!" Fitz declared. "It's like it was made for him."

"It does look good on him," Kate said slowly. "But I don't understand what this means. I can't afford to pay even half his board, and once he starts showing—"

"Don't be a dork." Fitz pulled off the saddle and set it down. "We've still got the same deal as always. You take care of the riding and training, and I take care of the expenses and all that boring stuff. And bask in the glory of your show ring triumphs, of course."

Kate stroked Flame's nose as he nuzzled at her. Fitz was acting like this was some casual transaction—nothing of any more consequence than buying her dinner. And maybe to him it was. But Kate couldn't quite force herself to think that way. Owning a horse—even half a horse? That was a responsibility she wasn't sure she was ready to handle. Sure, she'd dreamed of her own horse for most of her life. She and Nat had spent countless hours back in their barn rat days discussing exactly what kind of horses they wanted—how tall, what breed, what color. The specifics were always changing, but Kate knew none of her imaginary ponies could ever measure up to the real live horse standing in front of her.

And in a way, Fitz was right. The plan hadn't really changed. All along, Kate had been the one in the saddle bringing Flame along, training him, helping him reach his potential. For a second Kate allowed herself to feel excited as she thought of it.

Then she remembered—all that was before she'd found out about the assistant trainer job. Would she still have time to work with Flame as much once she went full time? And what about all the showing Fitz kept talking about? How was she going to do that if Jamie expected her to stay home, teach lessons, order feed, and keep things running while the rest of the barn was on the road? Had Fitz even stopped to consider that?

"Well?" Fitz stepped forward, looking pleased with himself as he wrapped his arms around her. "What do you think?"

"It's, um, unbelievable." She clutched Flame's lead tightly with one hand while hugging Fitz back with the other, trying not to let him see or feel her unease. "Thanks."

"You're welcome." He bent and kissed her, and Kate kissed him back, trying to lose herself in the moment and forget about the future.

TWENTY

——— ——— ——— ——— ———

"Where'd Dani go?" Zara stood and grabbed a second slice of pizza out of the box laid out on the big, metal-bound trunk in the middle of the tack room. "Because if she doesn't get here soon, we'll be all out of pepperoni."

"I'm not sure." Summer licked her fingers.

"I saw her in the tack room a few minutes ago," Kate said. "She said she had something to do and might be late." She and Fitz were sitting in the corner on a couple of over-turned buckets. Zara smiled when she noticed they were right in front of the rack holding Kate's snazzy new saddle.

Zara returned to her seat on the bench beside Tommi. "Hope I didn't scare Dani off, outing her like that."

"Had to be done." Tommi looked up from her pizza. "She was out of control. I think she sees that now."

"Yeah." Zara picked at an oozing strand of cheese. "Anyway, guess that's all over now."

Tommi nodded. "It's kind of too bad, in a way."

"Huh?" Zara shot her a surprised look. "What are you talking about?"

Before Tommi could answer, Dani rushed in. "Okay, you guys," she said breathlessly. "Check this out."

She was holding her smartphone. Curious, Zara set down her pizza and wandered over. "What? Did you blog about all the scandal and intrigue at our post-lesson pizza party?"

Dani laughed, though it sounded a little nervous. "Not exactly. Here, read it."

Zara took the phone. Sure enough, the HorseShowSecrets blog was on the screen. But Zara's eyes widened as she scanned the first few lines.

The others were watching her. "What?" Summer asked.

"She wrote a post 'fessing up to being the blogger." Zara glanced briefly at Dani, who was staring at the ground, and then read on. "She's sorry, she apologizes to anyone she hurt, yada yada. And she's getting out of the blogging business."

"Really? You're not going to do it anymore?" Summer asked. "Why not? You could still write it under your own name." When Marissa shot her an incredulous look, Summer shrugged. "What? I kind of liked hearing what was going on at other barns and stuff."

"Nope, I'm definitely out," Dani said with a visible shudder. "Sorry, you guys. Are we okay?"

"We're cool," Zara said, handing back the phone.

"Yeah," Fitz added, while Kate, Tommi, and Summer nodded.

"Marissa?" Dani smiled uncertainly at her friend.

Marissa sighed and ran a hand over her eyes. "Maybe we should talk. Can we go somewhere?"

Dani just nodded, looking anxious, and the two of them hurried out of the room. Zara wandered over to rejoin Tommi.

"Think those two'll be okay?" Zara asked.

Tommi wiped her mouth with her napkin. "Eventually. Marissa's not the type to hold a grudge."

Zara hoped she was right. At her old barn in California, she'd mostly enjoyed when there was drama. Hell, she'd started half of it.

But Pelham Lane was different. She liked that everyone was all dorky and friendly and supportive. She liked it a lot, actually.

"So wait," she said, suddenly remembering something. "What were you saying before? About it being too bad the blog was done, or something? I thought you thought the blog was totally lame. You didn't seem too thrilled any of the times you were on it."

Tommi picked at a burned spot on her crust. "Yeah. I don't know. In a way Summer's right, though. It was kind of cool to have a place to get all the news from different barns and keep up with who's doing what at the shows. You know, all in one spot."

"Only half the stuff on there wasn't even true." Zara grimaced at the memory of that stupid rumor about Zac.

"I know." Tommi shrugged. "I'm just saying. Anyway, it's too bad Dani's probably the only person on the circuit who knows enough people to make it work. Well, except for Marissa, anyway." She smiled. "And I'm not seeing her keeping up with something like that every day."

Zara shoved the last bite of pizza in her mouth and chewed

slowly. It really was pretty cool that Dani had been able to connect with enough people to make the blog work—and to keep people guessing about who was doing it.

"You know," Zara said, "I met a lot of interesting people at Harrisburg while I was interviewing them about the blog. That was kind of fun. And I'm not shy. I bet if I tried, I could get to know just as many show people as Dani."

Tommi glanced up from her pizza. "What are you saying?" She sounded surprised. "Are you thinking *you* might want to take over the blog?"

"Maybe. Why not?" Zara thought about it. "I liked trying to figure out who was writing it. It was sort of like being a news reporter or something. Coming up with stories for the blog might be fun like that too, you know?"

"Okay." Tommi sounded dubious. "But Dani just told the world the truth about writing it. It's not like you could go back to being anonymous without everyone suspecting she was back at it. I'm not sure she'd go for that."

"Who said anything about being anonymous?" Zara was starting to feel excited about this whole idea. "Like I said, I'm not shy. Besides, I'd be doing it legit—no stupid untrue rumors and crap like that. Just news and, like, regular-type gossip. Probably a few opinions, too. It could be fun!" She jumped to her feet, feeling energized. "Think I'll snag another soda. Want anything?"

"No thanks."

Tommi watched Zara head over to the food, still a little surprised by what she'd just said. Then again, maybe she shouldn't be. Writing that blog was right in Zara's wheelhouse. She was pretty much fearless—she definitely wouldn't be afraid to stand up for her opinions. Plus she knew what it felt like to be the victim of gossip and rumors, so she'd probably be a lot more careful about that kind of thing than Dani had been.

Popping the last bite of pizza in her mouth, Tommi got up and wandered over to Kate and Fitz. "Hey, guys." She grabbed another bucket and sat down beside them. "So where'd you two disappear to after the lesson? I was afraid you'd ditched us and gone to the diner or something."

"Oh." Kate glanced at Fitz. "Um, we were just—talking. You know."

Tommi grinned. "Oops, sorry for asking, you two lovebirds. It's hard to find enough cuddle time at the shows, right?"

Kate blushed, and Fitz grinned back. "Something like that," he said. "But actually—"

"Excuse me, everyone!" Joy strode into the tack room, cutting off whatever Fitz was about to say. "Could I have your attention?"

Tommi glanced over, surprised by the serious tone of Joy's voice. Marissa and Dani slunk into the tack room behind her, both of them looking oddly sheepish. What was going on?

Summer was over by the pizza boxes, picking at the leftovers. "What's wrong, Joy?" she asked, sounding bored.

"I just happened to overhear these two talking out in the aisle." Joy glanced at Marissa and Dani. "I always knew it was hard to keep a secret around here, but I had no idea my personal life was all over the Internet." She put a hand on her belly.

Tommi gulped, and several of the others let out audible gasps. "Great," Fitz said. "Way to have a big mouth again, Dani."

"Sorry," Dani said in a small voice. "We didn't realize she could hear us."

Marissa nodded. "Yeah. Sorry."

"Never mind." Joy sighed. "I was going to make an announcement soon anyway. Yes, I'm going to have a baby."

"Congratulations," Summer spoke up. "Is it a boy or a girl?"

"I don't know yet." Joy shook her head. "Anyway, apparently there's also a rumor floating around that I'm leaving my job here. I just want to let you know that one's definitely not true. I love Pelham Lane, and I plan to be back here with all of you as soon as possible after the birth."

The entire room went silent. Tommi looked over at Kate, and she wasn't the only one. Kate's face had gone pale, and she was staring fixedly at her pizza.

Joy didn't seem to notice the reactions. "I will be taking maternity leave, of course," she said. "But only for a few months, if all goes well."

"Who's going to do your job while you're away?" Dani shot a curious look in Kate's direction.

"Jamie's already lined up a temporary sub," Joy said. "A young aspiring trainer from Europe who wants to learn the ropes of the US system."

"Really?" Summer looked interested. "How old? Guy or girl?"

Joy pursed her lips. "You'll have to ask Jamie about that when he gets back. I'm not totally sure of the details—and I wouldn't want to start any *rumors* that might not be true. Enjoy your pizza, guys." She turned and left.

Kate was stunned. She was vaguely aware of Fitz reaching out to take her hand.

"Sorry, babe," he said.

Kate couldn't respond for a second. What did this mean? She struggled to make sense of the way her entire world—her future—had just shifted and changed yet again.

"Kate?" Tommi sounded concerned. "You okay?"

Kate glanced at her, feeling like the world's biggest idiot. "You knew all along," she said numbly. "You said it wasn't going to happen."

Tommi looked stricken. "I just meant . . . I'm sorry, Kate. I wish I was wrong."

"You never said anything to Jamie, did you?" Summer asked.

"No!" A sharp flash of alarm cut through Kate's numbness. "Wait—do you think Joy knows? Is she going to tell him? Oh my gosh—talk about humiliating!" She could feel her face going bright red.

"No!" Marissa said quickly. "We didn't mention you at all, Kate. We were just, uh, discussing—"

"Arguing," Dani corrected with a wry smile.

"Okay, arguing," Marissa said. "About how Dani came up with some of the stuff she wrote. I was asking how she knew for sure Joy was definitely pregnant and definitely leaving Pelham Lane. That's when she came around the corner and we realized she'd heard us."

"Oh. Good." Kate wasn't sure what else to say.

Tommi was still watching her. "Listen," she said. "You know how I felt about the whole job thing. I'm not saying it would have been a good idea either way. But I wish at least you'd had a choice, you know?"

Kate nodded. Choices. All of hers seemed to be vanishing all of a sudden.

Or were they? As she turned her head, she caught a glimpse of her new saddle on the rack behind her. Okay, so Fable was gone. She wouldn't be riding him in the eq finals next year. But that wasn't the end of the world. Lots of people never even got near Indoors, and she'd already had a chance to ride there.

She smiled faintly, thinking back to those glorious moments in the ring with Porter. That had been one to remember, for sure.

And who said it couldn't happen again? Feeling Fitz's strong arm around her, she leaned into him, thinking of Flame. Now partly *her* horse. Who knew how far he might go?

"Kate?" Tommi still looked worried. "You all right?"

"Yeah." Kate smiled at her, suddenly knowing it was true. "I'm fine."

Okay, so maybe she'd never have all the advantages of someone like Tommi or Zara or Fitz or some of the others. But maybe that was okay.

Because now that she thought about it, Kate still had more—*much* more—than she'd ever dreamed she could when she climbed aboard that first shaggy pony all those years ago.

And that was good enough for her.

ACKNOWLEDGMENTS

I want to acknowledge every horse and pony I ever had the chance to compete with at Indoors. Thank you for all the hours spent trying to qualify, for putting up with my mistakes, for always trying your best, and for knowing when it was time to shine.

A special thank-you to Jetsetter ("Jet") and Diplomacy ("Henry"). Jet, thank you for giving me my first championship at an Indoor. You gave me the confidence to go back every year. Thank you for proving to me that I can do it if I try hard enough. Without that first win, I would have been tempted to give up other years. Henry, you taught me to work hard and to believe in myself, but also to never think too much of myself or take a class for granted, and of course to save the best for last. I will never forget the moment I first laid eyes on you and the way I lost my breath for a few seconds. As I always said to you, I knew when I met you that something special was going to happen.

Thank you also to all my friends at Spence. Thank you for always welcoming me back to school after a long weekend of showing as if I had never been gone, for being so supportive of my riding, and for making me feel included in everything that I missed while I was away at shows. Thank you for celebrating with me when I had a good show, for helping me forget and move on from a bad show, and for loving me just the same either way. I would never have made it through my junior career without you.

Georgina Bloomberg

Christian Oh

GEORGINA BLOOMBERG is the younger daughter of New York City mayor Michael Bloomberg. An accomplished equestrian, Georgina is on the board of directors of the Equestrian Aid Foundation, the United States Equestrian Federation, the Hampton Classic Horse Show, Animal Aid, and both the Bloomberg Family and Bloomberg Sisters foundations. She is an Equine Welfare Ambassador for the ASPCA, a member of Friends of Finn for the Humane Society of the United States, as well as a member of the HSUS Horse Council. In 2006, she founded the charity The Rider's Closet, which collects used riding clothes for those who are unable to afford them. Now run by Pegasus Therapeutic Riding, the program has enabled thousands of riders to stay in the sport and have the proper apparel and equipment. She is a graduate of New York University's Gallatin School of Individualized Study.

Georgina is donating a portion of her proceeds from this book to Gallop NYC.

.NE HAPKA has published many books for children
)ung adults, including several about horses. A lifelong
.e lover, she rides several times per week and keeps three
)rses on her small farm in Chester County, Pennsylvania. In
addition to writing and riding, she enjoys animals of all kinds,
reading, gardening, music, and travel.